FATAL FIXER-UPPER

A CHRISTIAN COZY MYSTERY OF MURDER, SUSPENSE, AND REALITY TV

A COZY CORNER MYSTERY

KATHLEEN GUIRE

FATAL FIXER-UPPER

A Cozy Corner Mystery
by Kathleen Guire

FATAL FIXER-UPPER

A Cozy Corner Mystery
by Kathleen Guire

CHAPTER 1
PLOT TWISTS AT THE COZY CORNER

I SLID out of bed and shuffled to the window. A fresh, sloppy snow had fallen over the street, giving everything the appearance of being frosted. It was perfect winter weather outside, even though it was March. It was as if winter were shaking its aging fist, saying "I will not go gracefully." I would admire it from here in my cozy apartment office.

I clicked a pod into the Keurig and turned on my desktop computer.

I stretched out my hands and interlaced my fingers. "Who do I need to kill today?"

Of course, there was no one to answer me except my labradoodle, Poirot, named after one of my favorite sleuths. Because no one could say it properly, Aunt Mary shortened his name to Rory. After a while, I made my peace with it and the name "Rory" stuck.

I turned on some Ella Fitzgerald and Louis Armstrong jazz and picked up my phone to alert my faithful dog walker that Rory needed to go out.

Then I sat down with my coffee to get to work.

So far in the mystery I was writing, I had the setting and the main characters — that part was easy — because I'd been writing this series for five years. This was installment number ten. When you wrote the tenth in a cozy mystery series, it was difficult to figure out who to kill. Cozy mysteries often took place in small towns. It was no secret that I'd used the very town that I lived in, Evergreen Heights, as my setting.

I hadn't visited many other places except for that summer I spent in Europe with my parents when I was twelve. Together, they ran a successful and profitable arts acquisition company and traveled the globe all year. For that reason, I stayed with my aunt, who raised me because, like her, I was a homebody. That summer in Europe had been the most terrifying and lonely season of my life. The only bonus was the coffee. I loved it. Since then, I'd been a coffee snob, as my Aunt Mary said.

When I arrived home from the trip, my classmates were jealous and so was my seventh-grade history teacher. He made me give a presentation including a PowerPoint of the historic sights of Paris in front of the entire class. I did it, shaking the whole time, followed by a panic attack in the hallway. The nurse phoned my Aunt Mary to come and pick me up.

After a few more panic attacks at school, Aunt Mary pulled me out altogether and homeschooled me. I spent most of my time here in The Cozy Corner Bookstore. The bookstore she deeded to me when I turned twenty-five, the same year I wrote my first cozy mystery, *Cappuccino Chaos at Cozy Corner*.

FATAL FIXER-UPPER

A Cozy Corner Mystery
by Kathleen Guire

With the help of my mother, I converted the third and fourth floors of the white brick building into my living quarters. I worked in my office on the top floor, with large windows overlooking the historic downtown of Evergreen Heights. Then, when it was time for the bookstore to open, I headed down to the first two floors and worked for the day.

Back to who to kill. The problem with writing cozy mysteries is that being set in a small town, there are only so many people you can kill without the population becoming sparse. So for this tenth mystery, I brought in an imaginary film crew, actors, and staff. Instead of murdering a townsperson, I would kill a member of the film crew. Our town was very Hallmark-ish, so it fit the bill for a romcom-type mystery. I was thinking of entitling it—*Beaus and Bones at Birchwood Historical Society*.

My aunt and mother were active in our town's historic society, which meticulously kept up the shops on our historic main street, including my bookstore, the Cozy Corner, complete with a coffee cafe. Our town boasted the ever-famous romcom pavilion in the town square.

While I was building a scene, the doorbell buzzed on the floor below me. Poirot leaped off the reading chair he had been lounging on and slid across the hardwood floor toward the stairs. The perfect thing about my dog walking arrangement was that I didn't have to get up and answer the door. My employee Ben, who lived just across the street above a small organic grocery that his parents owned, walked across the street every morning, came upstairs, rang the bell, and punched in the code. Rory, being conditioned like Pavlov's dog, heard the bell and ran to answer the door all on his own while I stayed holed up in my office and worked. I had Rory's leash hanging by the door, so there was never any need to bother me.

Ben yelled, "Good morning, boss!" and left.

After Rory's walk, Ben and Rory hung out in the bookstore. Ben was my bookkeeper, so he had plenty to keep him busy until the bookstore opened at 8, even though the cafe portion of Cozy Corner opened at 6. He worked until noon, when he went back across the street to help his parents keep their books and handle the afternoon rush. 8 a.m. is an unusual time to open a bookstore, but it was something my Aunt Mary had insisted on when I was growing up. Moms with small children have been up for hours by the time 8 a.m. rolls around.

So, not only did we officially open the bookstore at 8, but our first story time was at 8, followed by another one at 8:30, and the final morning one at 9. Each story time could have anywhere between one and five kiddos, which made it easier to spend time with each child. We hosted an afternoon weekly book club for middle schoolers and another for high schoolers. Those were more heavily attended, especially when we spent a month on a suspense or mystery title. Not to mention, the book club for adults once a week was a reason to dress up, eat yummy snacks, and catch up with friends. Sometimes we talked about the book.

"The bookstore should be a community hub," my Aunt Mary said when I was growing up.

I had slid seamlessly into my role here and all the

activities. I'd never had a panic attack in my building. It was my safe haven. I loved the kids, talking about books, helping customers find just the right reads, and writing books. My life was almost perfect.

Almost, because there was still a lot of tension with my parents. Oh, they loved me, and I loved them. I was fine with them living their lifestyle. Mom came to visit when she could. Dad was stuck on "What is wrong with Harper?"

My aunt simply stated that I was wired differently and that I should be left alone. My dad finally ended all the sessions after they suggested his abandoning me caused my anxiety and agoraphobia. That's what I had. Sometimes I felt as if I should wear a T-shirt with the word emblazoned across my chest. Other times, I didn't feel broken. I felt at home in my building, and I loved my life. Of course, there were niggling questions at night, like how would I get married and have children? But I pushed those down like the espresso in the press and ignored them as best I could.

Instead, I focused on running my bookstore and writing books.

Mom had sent the gift of an e-bike so I could navigate the town. I didn't drive, and Aunt Mary didn't push it when I was sixteen, seventeen, or even when I did college classes online. The bike suited me just fine. With the bike, I could do my errands within half an hour and then get back home. I zipped around running errands like Angela Lansbury from *Murder She Wrote*, one of my aunt's favorite TV shows and my introduction to mystery shows. It was Angela who got me hooked on the cozy mystery format.

When my first book manuscript was complete, *Cappuccino Chaos at Cozy Corner*, Dad was determined to find me a publisher.

"I'm not using a publisher," I said. "That's old school, Dad."

"What do you mean? How are you going to publish?" he said at our weekly FaceTime meeting. I called it a meeting and recorded it that way on my calendar unless it was just Mom when Dad was busy. Mom and I made ourselves coffee and pretended we were meeting in a cafe. Sometimes I went downstairs to the bookstore cafe to make it feel as if it were really true. She told me about the latest art piece, and I talked about the bookstore and my latest book. Sometimes, she helped me figure out some plot issues. One of my novels centered on an art piece and the local museum. She helped me a great deal with the descriptions and art history.

"Dad, I'm going to self-publish, that's the way to go nowadays. I retain all the rights and all royalties go to me."

"Oh," he said. All the huff deflated in a moment of revelation. "At least let me set up an LLC for you," he said.

"Of course," I said. But I knew I hadn't heard the end of the publishing suggestion. I'd probably have a publishing agent show up at my bookstore, which I did. Nine, to be exact, but I turned them all down.

My phone buzzed and slid across the plexiglass of my desk. It was time for me to get dressed and go downstairs to the bookstore, and I still didn't know who to murder.

. . .

At five till eight, someone pounded on the Cozy Corner Book's door. Rory ran to the door, tail and body wagging as if he could unlock it. I followed behind. Aunt Mary and my best friend since childhood, Sage, pressed their faces against the glass, hands cupped, peering in.

"Good morning," I said as I typed in the code to unlock the door.

"Did you forget I'm leading story hour today?" Aunt Mary asked.

"I'm taking photos today for the paper and for you," Sage said, shaking the snow off her coat and stomping her feet.

Directly behind them were two families of regulars for the story hour. Instead of making them wait until the regular opening time, I welcomed them in.

"I bet you two would like some hot chocolate before story hour," I said to the two three-year-olds. "On the house," I offered to the two moms, who were busy peeling layers off the kids while trying to hold baby carriers. Aunt Mary and Sage stepped in to help. The moms, Clare and Ashley, were here almost every morning, so the kids—Theo and Dominic—were at home here. Once free of their snow gear, they ran to the counter and climbed up on stools, waiting for hot chocolate.

My barista Zoe had run across the street to grab baked goods from Bea's Bakery, so I made the hot chocolate, adding some marshmallows after I used an ice cube to cool it before I poured them into espresso cups. The baked goods selection was pretty poor. If the kids wanted a muffin, they would have to wait until Zoe arrived. Every morning, she stopped at the bakery across the street and picked up our order for the day.

As Aunt Mary breezed past me carrying a car seat with Clare's baby Audrey, who was sleeping peacefully, Mary whispered, "I have some big news to tell you after story hour."

Clare and Ashley had joined us at the counter. Sage followed Aunt Mary to the back of the shop with her camera equipment and the other car seat holding baby Peregrine, who was also sleeping peacefully.

"Zoe not in yet?" Clare asked while tightening her messy bun. "I didn't get much sleep last night. I could use some espresso."

As if on cue, the doorbell jingled and Zoe yelled, "Sorry, boss, I have the baked goods. The bakery was like Grand Central. There's a film crew here for something. I only got half of our order. Bea said she'd deliver more later."

Bea, the bakery owner, also served coffee, so if there were out-of-town guests, like a film crew…wait, maybe my story was coming true before my eyes. Maybe it was Hallmark, and they were taking advantage of our freak winter weather to film a Christmas movie. The weather wasn't actually freaky for us. Here on a mountain plateau, we often had snow as late as May. Summers were shorter and cooler, with an average temperature of seventy-five.

I didn't have time to pursue the Hallmark movie line of thought because while Aunt Mary wrangled Theo and Dominic, I picked *A Snowy Day* for today's read. Sage unpacked her camera and snapped photos of the process.

"Just pictures of the kids," I said. "Not me."

"The newspaper is writing a story about story hour. You're part of that," she said, running her hands through her ultra-slick blonde hair, a stark contrast to my blonde fuzzy coils. There was a time I was jealous of her five-eleven willowy figure compared to my five-foot-six, eat-a-muffin-and-gain-five-pounds figure. The depth of our friendship buried feelings of jealousy. She'd stuck by me all the years of my childhood when I suffered from anxiety and panic attacks. When other kids judged me, she confronted them. Once she got kicked out of high school for punching a classmate who called me names.

Sage owned her own photography studio five blocks away. She had a degree in forensic photography and helped the police on cases, but in a small town, it wasn't often they needed her. She also did work for the local newspaper when they needed her. "Multiple streams of income" was a motto she'd pounded into my head. No one can do just one thing anymore to really make a living.

I'd taken her advice to heart when I'd agreed to take over the bookstore, continue writing books, make the building my residence so I didn't have to pay for a house, and also run an online bookstore. I loved supporting self-published authors and dedicated an entire section to them, much to my father's chagrin. I emailed indie authors I followed when they released a new book, offering them a book signing at my shop.

I enlisted the help of Clare and Ashley while the

babies slept to assemble a craft for after the boys finished listening. We didn't always do crafts after story time, but I felt as if this day needed snowflake crafts. Although it snowed often in March here in the mountains, that didn't mean it was easy for everyone who hoped for warmer weather. Ashley and Clare helped me prep crafts for all three story times and ended up staying for two of them. Both babies woke during the second story time. Clare and Ashley took them upstairs to the comfy couches to nurse them while Dominic and Theo followed Aunt Mary like baby ducks.

At 9:30, after the last of the kids left, we had a slight lull. We'd ended up having fifteen kids over the three story times.

"That was great," Sage said. "I got so many pictures! I'll have some printed for you to hang up in the shop." She smiled as she stuffed her blonde locks into a black beanie. "Gotta run. Aunt Mary and I have an important photo shoot."

Sage had called Mary "Aunt" when she was four, and it stuck. No one could talk her out of it or get her to be more formal with Mrs. Hearst. Nope. Aunt Mary.

"Wait," I said, as Aunt Mary donned her red wool coat. "What photo shoot?"

"That's what I wanted to tell you!" she said, hugging me. "I signed a contract for a television series."

CHAPTER 2
THE COZY CORNER CONNECTION

"SO THE FILM crew is here for you?" Zoe yelled and squealed as she ran from behind the counter, her ebony spiral curls bouncing with joy.

"Yes," Aunt Mary said, clapping her hands. "I'm so excited."

Aunt Mary had signed the building and business over to me, not so she could retire, but so she could use her design degree. She followed a similar style to one of her favorite home shows. She used her own money to fix a house that the owners wanted to sell. At the reveal, she gave the owners the opportunity to sell it or pay her back the investment money and stay. She had expected all of them to sell. Her expectations were proved wrong when ten homeowners in a row decided to stay.

"The Home. Health. Family. Network called me after the tenth homeowner chose to stay and offered me a show." Aunt Mary smiled and turned to Zoe. "This contract is as much yours as mine. If you hadn't managed my social media for me, no one would have known I existed."

Zoe managed Aunt Mary's social media, making sure to post several photos a day on Instagram. Although Sage was the professional photographer, she only provided photos for Zoe to post occasionally. Most of the time, Zoe took candid shots or filmed reels and provided captions with calls to action to bolster engagement for Aunt Mary's account.

Zoe jumped up and down. "I can't believe it."

"Come on, Aunt Mary," Sage said. "I'll send you some photos and videos to post, Zoe!" she said as she dragged Aunt Mary out of the shop.

Zoe and I ran to the front windows to watch them hop into Sage's green jeep and drive away. Then it was back to work. I had another chapter to write upstairs in my office. Because of the film crew being in town, the lull might have been longer than usual. There was a group of retired men who came in every day at 10 a.m. for coffee, pastries, to talk about books, politics, and reminisce. I'd set an alarm to come down and greet them. That left me with forty-five minutes to write.

"You know what I need, Zoe," I said.

"Coming right up," Zoe said. "I can't believe you can write at a time like this. I'm too excited," she said as she pressed espresso into the portafilter basket using a tamper. "I heard your aunt is remodeling the Vanderhilt mansion on the edge of town. That place is massive."

"I'm taking Rory for a walk," Ben said as he exited the hallway leading to the back office where he did the bookkeeping. He grabbed the leash. Rory bounded across the store, wagging his tail.

"Aren't you excited?" Zoe called after him.

"Sure, yeah," Ben said, his head bowed.

As he exited, a customer came in. I wanted to make a quick exit, but with no one else on the floor and Aunt Mary gone, I needed to greet the customer.

My brain had already switched gears. I was thinking about two things: What was going on with Ben? And how did I conquer the plot of the current book?

Zoe rescued me by calling out, "What can I get you today?"

"Oh, thank you. I'll take a Lavender Honey Iced Latte."

"Gabrielle?" I said.

"Oh, Harper, it's been a minute."

By minute, Gabrielle meant she'd never set foot in the Cozy Corner Bookstore. From what I'd heard, she traveled an hour to the city to go to trendier places. I'd gone to school with Gabrielle until I was homeschooled. She was from the poorer side of town, having a mother who landed in jail on and off, and a father who abandoned her. Gabrielle persevered and became one of the popular teens when her grandmother stepped in and took over raising her. Gabrielle had married a Vanderhilt, the one who owned the very mansion my aunt was remodeling for her pilot episode.

"Shouldn't you be on set?" Zoe blurted out.

Gabrielle looked as if she were ready to be on camera with her butter-yellow wool coat and matching slacks. Her red hair was bobbed and styled to perfection.

"Oh, not yet," she gushed. "They will actually film the homeowners next week."

Zoe handed her the order and I expected her to turn and leave. Instead, she linked arms with me and said, "Can you give me a tour?"

I guess writing this morning was out the window. I gave her a tour. She smiled and commented on the woodwork and cozy couches upstairs. "I love how you have kept the historic aspects of the building yet modernized it."

"Thank you. My mom and Aunt Mary helped me with the changes," I said as we crested the stairs to the second floor.

"They are both in the historical society?" she asked. "My husband's uncle Eustace is on the board," Gabrielle added.

I sat on one of the Chesterton sofas, hopefully signaling the impromptu interview was over. "Yes, Eustace did the final review of the building and my apartment."

"Your apartment?" she asked, her brows arching.

"Yes, I live on the top two floors of the building," I said leaning forward like my father did, to indicate the conversation was over.

"May I see?" she asked.

"Of course," I said, while I wondered what in the world was going on. In grade school, I often shared my lunch with the underweight, unkempt version of Gabrielle. When Aunt Mary pulled me out of public school and my peers entered high school, Gabrielle transformed herself with the help of her grandmother and she never spoke to me again until today.

Once upstairs, Gabrielle oohed and aahed over my two-story apartment. The third floor of the building had an open floor plan with a kitchen/dining area open to the living room with a fireplace. Off to the side, I had a laundry/half bath area.

"Wait," Gabrielle said as she admired the fireplace. "Is this the same chimney for the fireplace on the first and second floors?"

"Yes, it was part of the original building. Your uncle Eustace insisted we use the original design as much as possible," I said, wondering why this mattered to her all of a sudden.

She twirled around to face the kitchen. "But your kitchen is so modern. I love your green cabinets and white granite countertops. Is that stove an antique?"

"No, it's a remake," I said. "My aunt helped me with the design. I love the old stoves and this is a copy with all the modern conveniences." It was true. I loved the orange range, and it complemented the green cabinets.

We headed to the second floor of my apartment, which was the fourth floor of the building. My building.

Again, Gabrielle was thrilled with the design, including the open feel with my bedroom, en suite, and office stretching across the front of the building. "Did you really need these double doors for your office?" she asked. "Why not leave it open? You never have anyone over."

For some reason, that last statement stung. I didn't know why. It was true. The only person who ever came up here to my bedroom/office was me. Just me. Not that I was looking to bring men up here. If I did date anyone, there wouldn't be anything happening up here. I was a firm believer that sex was reserved for inside the confines of marriage.

"We all know about your little problem."

Anytime someone puts the word "little" in front of a compliment, it is instantly degraded to an insult. I didn't know which of my many problems she was referring to. I'm sure she was referring to agoraphobia, which some people erroneously assumed meant a limited brain capacity. As if not being able to leave my safe zone meant I was brain damaged.

"That's true," I said. "I need doors because that's where I do some dictation for my books."

"Oh, yes, your aunt told me you had written a bunch of books."

"Yes," I said, unsure of how to end this conversation and get Gabrielle out of my apartment, my store, and my life. Period.

When we descended the stairs to my main floor, rather than heading for the door, she plopped down on the sectional and sipped her Lavender Honey Latte. "Any way I can get a refill?" she asked, settling deeper into the sofa.

"Absolutely," I said. I opened the apartment door and ran down the stairs before she could say another word.

"What is she doing up there?" Zoe asked as the espresso machine hissed. Before I could reply, she added, "I heard Mr. Vanderhilt's uncle Eustace is giving them all sorts of restrictions for the remodel of his late brother's home and using the historical society as an excuse to impose them."

"Really? I didn't find Eustace difficult to work with when we did the remodel here."

Eustace was old school. He wore a bow tie and suit

at all times, even when walking his bulldog Bruce. He was quiet and meticulous, burying himself in historical documents at his law office when he wasn't representing a big corporate client.

"That's because your aunt and mother knew all the guidelines and stuck to them." She waved her arms around at the heavy walnut beams and copper-plated ceiling. "You took the old shell, polished it up, and threw a café in here."

"Well, the counter was here," I said, grabbing a towel and wiping the counter. "This used to be a Maple Street Pharmacy & Soda Fountain, the place to hang out, back in the day."

"Exactly. What I've heard is that folks who don't follow the golden rules of Eustace get buried in legal papers until they give up," she said while setting down the latte and adding a plate with a pastry.

I took both and headed back up the stairs, my clue-finding brain on alert. By the time I'd reached Gabrielle, I think I'd figured out why she was here.

As I handed her a fresh latte and set the pastry plate down on the coffee table, I asked, "Is your husband's uncle Eustace making the remodel difficult?"

She looked at me, wide-eyed with surprise.

"I write mysteries, Gabrielle. You didn't think I'd figure it out? You ignored me from the time we started high school, and now you show up in my home and business asking about the historic society."

She straightened and crossed her legs. "Yes, he is. He doesn't want us to sell the house, so he is making remodeling it almost impossible."

"You seemed a little more upbeat after seeing my apartment."

"I am," she said, taking a nibble of her pastry. She swallowed and said, "I mean, look at your apartment, it's gorgeous and has all the modern touches I want."

"Well, I'm glad my brief tour and our conversation helped you," I said. "But I have to go back downstairs. I have some important customers coming in a few minutes."

"Of course," she said. "Thank you. I do feel better." She stood. "And Harper, I'll never forget you sharing your lunch with me. I'll never tell anyone and I'll deny it if you mention it. But I'll never forget," She slung her expensive handbag over her shoulder as she left my apartment.

I ushered Gabrielle downstairs, carrying her empty plate. I expected her to leave while I greeted the retirees, whom I secretly called "The Classics." I had blurted out the name one day while serving their coffees, and it stuck. Now they called themselves "The Classics" and corrected me if I didn't greet them by that name.

The Classics removed their coats, hats, and scarves. Dr. Dennis straightened his plaid bow tie before sitting down, his slick silver hair shone and boasted of another era. Robert threw his tan trench coat over the back of the chair, revealing a brown tweed suit you'd imagine seeing at Cambridge in England, not a small town like Evergreen Heights. Robert's flaming red curls fringed with the snow white of wisdom released like springs when he removed his hat and sat it on the table.

Edgar, the most vocal of the group, said, "I see you're mixing with the higher class, Harper." He nodded toward Gabrielle, who was browsing the table with my books near us.

Edgar had been a regular fixture in my life since Aunt Mary started homeschooling me. He wasn't retired then and still taught classes at the college. Every Tuesday and Thursday, he came into the Cozy Corner for some coffee between late afternoon and evening classes. I'd taken the opportunity to ask him a few questions about my homework one day while asking him if he'd like a refill.

After I served him his second cup of black coffee, he patted the seat next to him and said, "Let's look that up." After a few weeks, it became our Tuesday/Thursday study session until I took over the bookstore and he joined The Classics.

"Not sure why she is suddenly mixing with me," I said, using his words.

"You're smarter than that," Edgar said, patting me on the arm.

I gazed at perfect Gabrielle browsing the shelves. "The historical society."

"Bingo," he said.

"What are we talking about?" Robert asked.

Edgar jabbed his pointed elbow in Gabrielle's direction.

Robert narrowed his eyes and pushed his glasses up on the bridge of his nose. "I remember her. My wife used to save some dinner for her when she was no more than a street waif."

"Well, she's a Vanderhilt now," Edgar said. "And Harper's Aunt Mary is remodeling their family home on that new home show of hers, Sell It Or Stay."

"Oh," said the other three men in unison.

"You think she's only re-friending me because she wants me to put a good word in with the historical society."

"Now, you're thinking like a sleuth," Edgar said.

Just then, Gabrielle wiggled past the table, balancing nine books—all of them mine. The top two books slipped, and Edgar reached out and caught them.

"Let me help you with that," Edgar said. He was looking at me, not her. He winked.

"I'm going to catch up on all your books, Harper," Gabrielle said as she headed toward the counter, following Edgar.

"Harper hosts a book club every Thursday night," Robert said. I jabbed him in the side with my elbow.

"What?" he said.

Gabrielle paid for her books, waved, and left.

I chatted with The Classics for a few more minutes before I headed upstairs with Rory to write. It was now 11 a.m., and I hadn't written one word. I made myself an omelet instead of heading straight to my office. Ben left at noon, so I didn't have a whole lot of time. I decided to ditch writing for the day and check on Ben.

After finishing my brunch, I went back downstairs. While I looked for Ben, I couldn't stop thinking about Gabrielle and the historical society. Did she really think I had any pull? My aunt and my mother had strong personalities. I didn't have strong anything—not opinions, not powers of speech, not political power. I pretty much didn't have any strengths. I knew the townsfolk (I'd been hanging around The Classics too much) talked about me and, as Gabrielle had said, "my little problem."

I was a bundle of problems. I couldn't handle being outside of my building for longer than half an hour. If I hit the twenty-eight-minute mark while running errands, my surroundings blurred, my heart pounded as if it were going to come out of my chest, and dark circles floated in my peripheral vision. If a neighbor happened to stop me on the street when I was in what Aunt Mary and my therapist called "the red zone," I could pass out. It was the body's way of protecting itself from harm.

My mom and aunt had read many books on trauma with and for me. The only problem was, I didn't think I had any deep trauma. I felt secure with my Aunt Mary. My mother was loving. My father said this trauma stuff was all hogwash, but that's my father. I still went to therapy once a week, virtually, but I didn't feel as if I needed it.

As long as I lived in my safe zone, I enjoyed my life and that was enough for me. I didn't want to constantly entertain the idea that I was broken and needed to be fixed. But that's what the whole town thought. Gabrielle had just proven that in our short encounter, ending with a pity purchase of all my books, which she would probably throw in the trash when she got home.

I set aside my thoughts and went in search of Ben. I found him in the small back office, hunched over the computer.

"Don't tell me our numbers are down," I said.

"No, everything is on track."

"Then what's up?" I asked.

"What do you mean?" he said, standing and stretching his arms and yawning.

"You've been acting funny all day. Normally when you walk Rory, you stop in the cafe to flirt with Zoe." I smiled. "Today you just zipped right past her."

"I don't want you to be mad at me," he said, bowing his head, his dark bangs covering his chocolate eyes.

I couldn't imagine what I would be mad at Ben for. He kept our books meticulously, helped his parents run their organic grocery in the afternoons. If there was an award for all-around best kid, it would go to him. But he wasn't a kid anymore. He had graduated college two years ago and then taken his CPA exam. Yet, here he was, still doing the same job for me he had for the past four years when he came on as an intern.

"You want to take another job."

"I hate when you do that," he said, shuffling back and forth on his feet.

"What?" I said, genuinely surprised.

He scratched his head, messing up his mop of black hair. "Use your superpower on me."

"Superpower," I laughed.

"Well, finish," he said. "Say 'here's what happened' or something."

He was referring to Adrian Monk, the defective detective from the television series. For some reason, today this felt like a jab instead of a compliment. I knew he meant nothing by it, but I felt as if I'd been stung by five bees. All I wanted to do was run back upstairs and hide in my office. I'd never had a panic attack in my building. Yet, here I was, trying to catch my breath, black dots swimming on the edges of my vision.

"Harper! Are you okay?" Ben's voice sounded hollow and far away.

"You're leaving me," I said. I plopped down hard on the wooden chair behind me and put my head between my legs and took a few deep breaths.

Ben ran from the room and came back in with Zoe, who was talking to someone on the phone.

"Don't call 911," I said, finally getting a deep breath.

"I called your Aunt Mary," Zoe said. The Classics now crowded in the doorway, blocking off all the air in the building.

Edgar stepped forward with a glass of water.

"Everyone out," he said. "Harper needs space and air."

Everyone complied. "Your aunt is on the way," Zoe yelled as Ben hauled her out of the office.

"It's all my fault," he said from the hallway.

"Let's take some deep breaths," Edgar said. "Sip this water."

Edgar was a behavioral science professor in his former life, as he called it. I felt safe with him on one hand, but on the other hand, he was probably going to analyze my behavioral patterns.

After five minutes of breathing in for four seconds, holding four seconds and exhaling for four seconds, I could stand, and the anxiety was subsiding.

"He told you about the job," Edgar said.

"He tried," I said weakly.

"I thought his news might trigger you. That's why I asked The Classics to stay a little extra long today.'

I used my arm as a kickstand as I leaned on the desk trying to look composed and normal. "Trigger me?'

Edgar looked me full in the face with sympathy swimming in his chocolate brown eyes. "Yes, people leaving you triggers your childhood wounds."

"That's ridiculous," I said, pushing myself off the desk. My legs quivered, and I sat back down.

"Where's the job?" I said, changing the subject.

"It's in the capital. He'll be working for the city, which means a significant pay increase and a move."

"Oh, he is leaving."

"He grew up, Harper," he said, patting me on the head.

"I never grew up. I'm still here," I said with my head in my hands.

Edgar folded his long lanky frame and squatted next to me. He patted my head as if I were Rory needing some love and attention. "Of course you grew up. You run a successful bookstore. You've written nine books. Those sound like grown up accomplishments to me."

"I'm afraid, Edgar," I said, grabbing his arm and squeezing it. "I've never had an episode in my own building."

"You've had several triggers today. Your aunt is signed to host a show on the Home. Health. Family. Network. Gabrielle. And now Ben."

"Oh," I had nothing else to say.

"Maybe this building is not your safe place."

"Don't say that," I said, tears streaming down my cheeks. "I have to have a safe space."

He stood. "That's not what I meant. Maybe you need to address your trauma triggers."

"I don't understand. I've never had any trauma."

Edgar patted me on the head again. "I'm sorry, dear,

this isn't the time. Sip your water. I'll go grab you a cinnamon roll."

"Wait," I said, as he froze, framed in the doorway. "Could you be my therapist?"

"I'm not a therapist," he said.

"I know. But you know me. You know my 'patterns of behavior' as you call them. My therapist isn't helping me at all. Please. I'm tired of being broken."

"You're not broken," Edgar said. "The things that happened to you aren't you." And he left.

Minutes later, he re-entered the office, set down my cinnamon roll. "I'll do it," he said. "On one condition: you do exactly what I ask you to."

Before I could agree, my Aunt Mary rushed in and said, "Are you okay, Harper?"

CHAPTER 3
ODD GIRL OUT AT THE COZY CORNER

IT HAD BEEN a month since Aunt Mary's film crew from Home. Health. Family. Network began taping the pilot episode of Sell It Or Stay.

"Don't forget, we get to be on set today," Zoe said as she took my empty coffee cup. "In an hour."

Today was week four of the Vanderhilt mansion remodel. While I had made progress in my journey with tiny victories, Aunt Mary had had a tough month. The tension between Horace, Gabrielle's husband, and Eustace had created many arguments, causing delays in the remodel and taping. Horace had not followed the homeowners' agreement and stayed off the property. Instead, he had shown up at the house and demanded changes that didn't fit the budget or the historical society's guidelines.

I had been working with Edgar a few times a week. His brand of therapy involved lots of journaling, pinpointing patterns of behavior, and then addressing each pattern. We had worked on exposing limiting beliefs, and as much as I hated to admit it, my parents, without realizing it, had inflicted some trauma. I had a deep sense of abandonment and shame. I certainly was not healed, but I had learned a lot about how trauma affected the body, behavior, beliefs, biology, and brain—the five Bs, Edgar called them. Two major outcomes of the month were that Edgar had stretched my half hour away from my safe building to an hour, and the second I wasn't sure about.

Edgar had suggested I take some online tests, which I did. "I think you're on the spectrum," he had said as he examined the results he had printed out. "I'd like you to see a psychologist friend of mine. This would answer a lot of questions," he had said, the last sentence more to himself than to me.

I had felt myself shutting down after the "autism" word. Instead of letting me sit, he had grasped my hand and said, "Let's see what you can read on the subject, so you feel better." One pattern Edgar had helped me recognize was when I was afraid or unsure of something, I shut down. The new behavior made me feel more in control—research—or he liked to call it, info dumping on a subject.

We had perused the shelves and found *Odd Girl Out* and *On the Spectrum*. He had left our session with me sipping coffee and reading *Odd Girl Out*.

My mother, who was serving as the art advisor on the set of Sell It Or Stay. She had come to visit with some pieces for the homeowners to choose from. Eustace had rejected them all because they weren't historically correct for the area. Horace had argued to keep them because he couldn't handle his uncle's meddling anymore. Mom had scurried around town looking through library articles and the local art books in my store, trying to keep the peace. She was used to appeasing foreign dignitaries, princes, and museum curators. She took the tension and arguments in stride and plowed through with a smile as long as she remained the center of attention and got some screen time on the show.

Aunt Mary had always been the epitome of grace and kindness. With her warm smile and twinkling eyes, she effortlessly drew people in. Known in the town for her readiness to lend a helping hand, Aunt Mary was the person everyone turned to in times of need. Her gentle voice and genuine interest in others' well-being made her beloved by all. However, beneath this warm exterior lay an unexpected and unsettling side.

In the blink of an eye, her demeanor could shift dramatically. Her once kind eyes could turn cold and piercing, and her soothing voice could become sharp and commanding. It was as if a dark cloud suddenly descended over her, transforming her from the friendly aunt into someone completely unrecogniz-able, clearly a side effect of the pressure of filming the show. This was not my Aunt Mary. This unpredictable change harmed not only her social media account and persona, but made people tread carefully around her, never quite sure which version of Aunt Mary they would encounter. The contrast between her two personas was stark, and the sudden shift from sweet-ness to harshness was both shocking and unnerving, like the sudden chill of a winter storm on a sunny day.

Eustace had said one day, "I'm shutting down the remodel. There are too many infractions."

"No you aren't. I have followed all of your guidelines. Don't forget I'm in the historical society as well. I know the rules."

On another day, when Horace had demanded some changes, she had said, "That means more money. Are you going to come up with more money? I didn't think so."

The fiery sparks on the set were exactly why tickets to taping were a sought-after item in the town. Zoe had been in a tizzy all month because she was Aunt Mary's social media manager and she felt as if the persona she had created had flipped from "nice Aunt Mary" to a modern-day Cruella de Vil.

She handed me my coat after flipping the sign on the door from open to closed.

"Don't we have another half hour?" I asked.

"Listen, your aunt has morphed her online persona from sweet-and-savvy to evil. Do you know how many photos others who attend the tapings are posting online of your aunt?"

She pulled out her phone. "Look at this…" She showed me a photo of my aunt with an angry expression and hashtags "#diva #evil #witch."

"Okay. So we need to get there and take some better photos?" I asked.

"Yes," she said as she shoved my arm in my coat sleeve as if I were a toddler instead of her boss. "Sage is there but she's focusing too much on the drama. She's going to ruin your aunt's online presence."

I had barely seen Sage for the past month. She had

been busy with the show, newspaper assignments, and spring photoshoots.

"How long are we staying?" I asked as I buttoned my coat.

"I've got that covered. Edgar says you need to add five minutes today. Your mom is going to bring you home when you've hit your limit."

"Okay," I replied. "Let's go."

Ten minutes later, Zoe left me sitting in a chair in a tent on set. Sage plopped down in a canvas chair beside me. "Hi, friend, you picked the wrong day to come."

"Why?" I asked.

"There were a few 'talk to the contractor' and 'design team decisions' on the docket, but Eustace filed an injunction and shut the whole project down," she explained, her voice tinged with frustration.

"What?" I blurted, leaning in closer.

"Horace added a hot tub to the list of improvements, which meant digging up the backyard to bury power lines or something." She frowned, shaking her head.

"The hot tub isn't historically accurate?" I asked, eyebrows raised in surprise, as I chuckled at my own joke.

"I don't think the 'historically accurate' part is the problem. The issue is he doesn't want it beside the pool. He wants the hot tub back there near the old conservatory." She gestured toward the back of the property, where the glass-walled conservatory stood, untouched by time.

"I love the conservatory. It looks historically accurate, so what's the issue?" I wondered aloud, glancing at the structure with admiration.

"The issue is that it hasn't been touched for over ten years. They would have to run not only new electrical lines, but also plumbing. Eustace vehemently opposes changing the conservatory. He shut down the project," she replied, crossing her arms as she stared at the conservatory.

"Wow," I murmured, standing up to get a better view of the conservatory. "It is a beautiful piece of history, but it could stand some updates," I added.

"Yes, you should have heard the argument earlier by the pool in the backyard between Eustace and Horace. Then your aunt got involved," she said, her voice lowering as she recalled the scene.

"What did they argue about?" I asked, curiosity piqued.

"I'll show you," she responded, pulling out her camera and clicking the play button. Eustace and Horace appeared on the screen.

"Do you not care about your father at all?" Eustace demanded, his voice taut and trembling with anger.

Horace's face mottled, turned a deep shade of purple, the veins in his neck throbbed visibly. "Of course I do. The question is, did he care about me? He left us, remember?" he shot back, his voice thick with emotion.

Horace was referring to the disappearance of his father on his twenty-first birthday, the day he had inherited the estate.Not to mention the attractive live-in housekeeper, Maria, had disappeared at the same time.

At first, the police had suspected foul play, but after sifting through all the facts and interviewing the family and staff, they had concluded that Clive and Maria had chosen to disappear. After all, the clues had pointed in that direction. The day before he had disappeared, on Horace's twenty-first birthday, Clive Vanderhilt had withdrawn three million dollars from the family bank account. Then he had disappeared. The police had decided he must have wanted to retire in some other country.

Eustace pointed a finger at Horace. "You killed your father because he wanted a measly three million and a relationship with a housekeeper." It had been ten years since that accusation had flown out of his mouth while he had been on camera with the local media.

"I didn't care about the money," Horace, young and full of grief, said. "I didn't mind that he was dating Maria, she was like a mother to me."

Horace had suffered the loss of two people he had loved in one day. His mother had died when he was two and he had attached himself to the housekeeper, who was much more than that to the family, according to Aunt Mary.

Horace had spent the next ten years hiring detectives to find his dad, scouring the globe for his father and his mother figure, to no avail. On the other front, he'd done everything to prove his uncle wrong, by marrying Gabrielle, who, despite her polished look now, had lived most of her childhood in the projects. He hadn't touched the Vanderhilt estate until then. He'd waited until he'd grown the fortunes even more and used his new money while leaving the Vanderhilt money alone.

The grief and pain of their loss turned Eustace and Horace into different creatures. Horace ruled his company with anger and bouts of violence, evident on the recording Sage showed me. He shook Eustace, holding on to his suit collar. Eustace, normally quiet and reserved, said, "You can't just leave the family home alone and preserve the memory of my brother?"

"My family home. Dad left it to me, not you." With that, Horace shoved Eustace into the freshly gleaming pool that had been opened for the reveal. It was still forty degrees outside.

Horace stomped away as the medics on the set pulled a sputtering Eustace from the pool.

"There's more," Sage said. "Honestly, I had no idea being on the set of a home renovation show was like those reality shows we love to hate so much."

Sage played another clip of my Aunt Mary and Horace. "You're going to finish this house. I don't care about the injunction. I can have my attorneys down here in a hot minute," he said as he advanced toward her, his features transforming into a likeness of a gargoyle on the front of the house.

Aunt Mary backed away, smoothing her trousers and pulling her shoulders back. "You get your attorneys down here and then we'll talk."

Horace moved so close to my aunt, his nose was practically touching hers. "You will do exactly what I say–"

Before he could finish, Aunt Mary said, "Or you'll throw me in the pool like you did with your uncle Eustace?"

"He deserved it," he said, spitting as Aunt Mary backed away a second time.

"I respect your uncle and all he has done for Evergreen Heights." She turned on her heel and walked in the direction of the coffee cart. "I'm not moving forward until the injunction is lifted."

Horace responded to her by throwing his phone, which instead of hitting her, bounced off the patio and landed in the pool.

"Wow, that's crazy," I said. "I thought being on set would be boring for you."

"Quite the opposite," Sage replied with a laugh.

"Don't you dare post those," Zoe said from behind my chair, where she had apparently sneaked up and watched the clips.

"I won't. I promise," Sage said. "I read you loud and clear. No photos or videos that don't have the Zoe stamp of approval." She shifted in her chair as if she were uncomfortable about what she had to say next. "Except for the ones the newspaper paid me for."

"What?" Zoe said. "Please Sage, don't do this to Aunt Mary."

"I'll try to help her online persona. But she isn't doing herself any favors right now," Sage said.

My thoughts were muddled at the moment. Eustace and Horace really knew how to push my aunt's buttons. Maybe she needed to talk to Edgar or my mom or someone other than me, whose main coping mechanism was to go home and shut down or write.

My next thought went to Gabrielle, who had attended my book club for the past four weeks in a row faithfully reading the chapters, which made me think she really needed a friend. If Horace was violent with his uncle and employees, how did he treat her?

———

"Nothing is happening on my house," Gabrielle said at the Thursday night book club. We'd finished our discussion and were sipping coffees and nibbling on cookies from the bakery across the street.

"That's a shame," I said.

"It's been two weeks and Eustace isn't budging," Edgar added.

"I don't want to move," Gabrielle said, with a sad smile. "Horace is determined to sell and get off the family property."

"Do you think he can't forgive his dad?" I asked. This digging up past trauma and how it affects us was all new to me. I'd been reading books and journaling about how being abandoned made me feel. My own examination opened my eyes to the fact that others around me might be going through some stuff as well.

"I think that's it. His dad leaving without a trace changed him," she said.

"I understand," I said.

After we wrapped up, Edgar pulled me aside. "Have you noticed Gabrielle always wears long sleeves?"

"Yes, I wondered about that." While everyone else had either removed cardigans or worn short sleeves during our lively discussions by the fireplace, Gabrielle tugged at her long sleeves making sure they covered her wrists. "Do you think Horace is violent with her?"

"We've seen his pattern of behavior in public, it's likely that it is worse in private."

"Oh," I said. I wasn't sure how to react. Sure my dad

had pursued his career instead of staying here in the United States with me, but he'd never been violent. I couldn't imagine what Gabrielle was going through. She not only had abandonment, abuse, and neglect in her past, but now some facets of it may be in her present. Gabrielle had become a good friend in the past month. She'd never asked me to use my relationship with my aunt or Eustace. She'd plugged in to the book club and loved discussing books with The Classics.

Some part of her had been awakened to the joy of reading for the first time.

"What should I do?" I asked.

"Don't do anything right now. Just be her friend. I'll call a few people and find out all I can."

By "some people," I knew he meant the police and the hospital. One of those "some people" had recently joined our book club. Detective Dexter. Dexter recently moved to town and as he mentioned at book club, he was "plugging into the community." I could ask him, but I'd let Edgar handle the one-of-the-book-club-members-might-be-in-an-abusive-relationship conversation.

CHAPTER 4
BOOKWORM AT THE COZY CORNER

AS GABRIELLE SLIPPED on her dusty rose colored trench coat, her blouse sleeve moved above her wrist for a microsecond and I saw purple bruising, like a bracelet around her wrist. She quickly adjusted it.

"Hey, Gabrielle, can you help me with something tomorrow?" I said, pretending I hadn't seen anything.

"Sure," she said. "What's up?"

"Well, I'm going to attempt a hike at Christmas Tree Forest."

"That's brave of you!"

Dexter lingered in the background, sipping coffee, and thumbing through one of my novels. Standing at an impressive six feet four inches, Dexter had a commanding presence that was hard to ignore. His muscular build, a testament to hours spent at the gym, was complemented by his dark, intentionally messy hair that framed his chiseled features. His square jawline gave his face a strong, defined look, and the square glasses perched on his nose added a touch of intellect to his otherwise rugged appearance. At book club, Dexter didn't give off a law enforcement vibe, instead he seemed relaxed in his pullover sweaters, corduroys, and hiking boots. His frame folded like my laundry rack, leaning precariously on the table. I pulled Gabrielle away from Dexter and my stack of books.

Why was he reading one of my books and why did that bother me? Didn't authors want readers? Sometimes I think in my small self-created world, I thought of the town as my readers and that's as far as my circle extended. Obviously, my sales numbers told a different story. Right now, I knew two things - I didn't want Dexter knowing about my agoraphobia or reading my books. Once I had dragged Gabrielle behind the cafe counter with the pretense of rinsing coffee mugs, I said,

"Thank you. I need a hiking buddy. Would you come with me?"

Honestly, I would normally ask Sage, but she'd been swamped. Between the home show, the injunction, and now switching to spring family photo shoots at her studio, she barely had a moment to breathe.

"Yes, I'd love to," she said, flipping her meticulously styled red bob over her collar.

"Do you have some hiking gear?" I asked, testing her hiking vibe. At the same time, I was still convincing myself I wanted to hike.

"No, but I can pick some up," she said with a giggle.

"Do you?" she asked, eyeing my retro purple dress.

I didn't. It was true, I wore a dress or skirt every day. It had become my bookstore owner's uniform. In fact, once I found the style of dress or skirt I liked, I ordered it in every color and pattern. Same with boots, cardigans, jackets, and shoes. My mom called it a capsule wardrobe.

"That was my next question. I don't have hiking gear either…"

"Oh, let me pick some up for you. I love to shop," she interrupted.

"I was going to go to Tom's Sporting Goods, but that would use my outing time."

"No need to explain," she said. "What time do you want to hike?"

"Three p.m. tomorrow?"

"I'll be here at two forty-five with your clothes and boots."

Letting someone choose hiking clothes and boots for me was so far out of my comfort zone, I felt as if I'd left the country and I was back in Paris and twelve years old.

I had to do it. I couldn't stay stuck anymore. I wanted to move forward in my healing journey.

After sharing my sizes with her, Gabrielle made notes on her phone and left.

I tentatively approached Dexter. "Hey, I need to close up and go home."

"Oh, yes, sure." Then he looked me full in the face for the first time. Our eyes locked for what felt like an hour but was probably only a microsecond. He smiled and his gaze shifted back to the book. He flipped to the back cover. He gazed at the photo of me, which was the product of a photo shoot Sage had arranged after scouring Pinterest for "author photo shoot ideas." My blonde curls were perfectly coiled, no frizz, no strays and my makeup was flawless, complimenting my blue eyes.

"This is you," he said. "You're an author."

"Yes," I answered, not sure what else to say.

"It's good," he said. "I'll take it."

That was it. "It is good" isn't exactly the compliment a writer likes to hear. It's worse than Darcy in *Pride and Prejudice* saying Elizabeth is tolerable. Authors spend countless hours plunking away on computers, weaving words to create a compelling story, a plot, and in my case, a mystery to solve. With my head down, I walked to the checkout counter and quickly rang him up, which consisted of him swiping his own card through the iPad setup. I looked everywhere except his face. I didn't know why his comment had upset me so much, as well as the gnawing knowing that I didn't want this tall handsome man to know about how messed up I was.

He wore a deep navy blue pullover, its thick knit providing warmth and a touch of sophistication. Underneath, he had on a simple white button-down shirt, the crisp fabric contrasting with the soft texture of the sweater. His corduroy pants, in a rich chestnut brown, were both comfortable and stylish, the perfect blend of casual and refined. On his feet, he sported a pair of well-worn leather hiking boots, their scuffed surfaces hinting at many adventures. The look was completed with his signature square glasses and a silver watch on his wrist, a classic timepiece that added an extra layer of elegance to his ensemble.

"Would you like me to walk you to your car?" he said, jolting me out of my self-deprecating reverie.

I shifted from one foot to the other, trying to figure out what to do with my body. How did one stand when alone with a man in a bookstore/cafe? "I don't have a car."

"You can't walk home alone. It's pitch black out," he said as he slipped his card back in his wallet.

"Oh," I said. "I'm fine." *I live upstairs because I'm an agoraphobic mess and by the way, I'm autistic. At least that's what the online test says and Edgar believes. Believe me, Dexter, you don't want anything to do with this Emily Dickinson-type recluse.*

Instead of leaving, he pocketed his receipt, turned, and walked back to a comfy chair and plopped down.

"What are you doing?" I said, following him.

"I'll wait with you until you are ready. Like I said, you shouldn't walk home alone."

Too stunned to say anything, I straightened a few books. Instead of telling the truth, I grabbed the remaining coffee cups and took them to the cafe kitchen, something Zoe promised to do in the morning. But I had to do something. How did I get this handsome man out of my bookstore without telling him the truth?

At that moment, Rory stirred from his dog bed in the corner, stretching and yawning. He let out a little yelp to tell me he needed to go out. Without saying a word, I grabbed his leash from the coat rack and clicked it on his collar. Dexter shifted his long frame and then stood. He grabbed his wool coat off the rack. "Ready?" he asked.

We walked out in silence. Dexter followed my lead as I let Rory stop and sniff, marking a few lamp posts before we arrived at the small park in the center of town where I unclicked the leash.

Rory ran around in circles and I smiled.

"He's having a good time, isn't he?" Dexter commented.

Then Rory stopped, sniffed, and sat down.

"He found a clue," I said. Before I could stop myself I was explaining Rory's real name, Poirot, how he got it, why it was shortened to Rory, and how I loved mysteries.

"I love mysteries too," he said.

"We should get back," I said, suddenly conscious of the fact that I was keeping the new detective out late under false pretenses.

"I thought I was walking you home," he said.

"I live above the bookstore," I said. My cheeks flamed hot and I hoped he couldn't see them in the lamplight.

"Ahhh," he said with a chuckle. "I guess my detective skills need some work."

"Sorry," I said quickly as Rory bounded up to me and sat while I clicked on his leash.

"Now, I will walk you home," Dexter said and walked me back to the door of Cozy Corner Bookstore.

After I punched the code in and opened the door, he said, "I'd like to talk more about your book *Espresso Espionage at Evergreen Books*. Are you free for coffee tomorrow afternoon?"

"No, I'm going hiking with a friend," I said, proud of the fact that I sounded like a normal person. Before I could stop myself, I said, "How about the following day?"

"Sounds good," he said. "Nice chatting with you, Harper. You astonish me." And he was gone, striding down the street, the lights bouncing off his coal black hair.

———

As I closed and locked the bookstore door, I did six rounds of box breathing. I can do this. I can do it. I can do all things through Christ who strengthens me. Where did that come from? I hadn't prayed or read the Bible for years, since I'd returned from Europe at twelve years old and my life imploded. Maybe it was time to get back to prayer.

My phone buzzed.

Aunt Mary:

The injunction will be lifted Monday.

Me:

Yay!

Aunt Mary:

Yes, I'm ready to finish this project.

Me:

I'm sure. It's been a difficult one.

Aunt Mary:

For sure. I am normally a nice person but Horace makes me want to kill someone.

Me:

Laugh emoji.

Aunt Mary:

I miss you! Hopefully, this will be over soon and things can get back to normal.

Me:

Miss you too. Goodnight.

True to her word, at two forty-five the next day, Gabrielle breezed into Cozy Corner, carrying bags from Tom's Sporting Goods.

"I bought several outfits so you can choose what works for you," she said. "I have the receipt and Tom says you can return whatever you don't want."

"Thank you!" I said. Gabrielle and I went upstairs to my apartment to change. She was still wearing her normal attire: a coat and matching slacks with heels and a long sleeve blouse.

Fifteen minutes later, we were wearing trekking shoes, waterproof jackets, hiking pants, and filling water bottles at my fridge while giggling like middle schoolers.

"What's going on?" Sage said as she entered my open doorway.

"Oh, Sage, hi," I said. "We're going on a hike."

"You?" she said. Sage had missed a lot of what was going on in my life the past six weeks. For Sage, I'd always been the friend that was here. By "here" I mean in my building while she lived life. Any time she needed me, she could drop by and I was here. That was changing with the treatment plan Edgar implemented.

Sure, I could only leave home for an hour and a half now, but that was more than Sage had ever seen me do.

"Want to come?" I asked.

"No, I can't. I have to edit some photos. I thought I could get your opinion on a few. So I came to Cozy Corner. Zoe said you were up here."

"Oh, sorry, I can't right now. I'm pretty booked for

the rest of the day." I giggled. "Get it, booked. I own a bookstore and I'm a writer. I'm booked."

Gabrielle laughed.

"Who are you and what have you done with Harper?" Sage asked and then stomped down the stairs.

I had no idea what I'd done to offend her. Whatever it was, it would have to wait. I wanted to enjoy this outing.

Five minutes later, we were in Gabrielle's Toyota Highlander heading the five minutes to the trail.

Unlike Sage, she wasn't giving me the sideways glance every minute to see if I was freaking out.

I didn't freak out. I enjoyed the short drive, watching landmarks whiz by that I hadn't seen in years. The hemlock forest was my favorite when I was a child. When my parents came home for Christmas, I begged them to take me to Christmas Tree Forest so I could play in the snow. The hemlocks heavy with fresh snow looked like Christmas trees and that's how the park got its name.

We pulled into the parking lot and I hopped out and put the backpack on me with my water bottle stuffed in the pocket. Gabrielle did the same. The temp was in the fifties, perfect hiking weather. After examining the trail map, we decided to take the two mile loop instead of the five mile trail. I'd conquer the longer trail another day.

The sun shone down on us, the days slowly stretching the light as spring advanced. A few minutes into the trail, I felt the familiar panic rising up my chest. No, I'm not doing this. I'm not quitting.

"Aren't your mom and aunt from a wealthy family

like the Vanderhilts?" Gabrielle asked as she picked up a pinecone. "I've heard rumors, but I don't know the real story."

"Oh, yeah," I said, catching my breath.

"Are we going too fast?" she asked, pausing on the trail.

"No, just a little anxious," I said. Why did I say that? I just proved to her that I was broken. What had she said the first day she came back into my life, *my little problem*?

"I struggle with anxiety too, but look at you! You're out here at a state park, hiking."

"Yes, I am," I said.

"Do you want to go back to the car?"

"No, I want to do this," I said. "My aunt and mom are from a wealthy family." Maybe telling their story, what I knew of it, would help me regulate.

"I don't know what family. They changed their last name."

"Oh," she said.

"Their dad was abusive. But no one would believe it. Aunt Mary is three years older than my mom. She tried to protect my mom. When Aunt Mary turned twenty-one, she received a trust fund from her mother. The day she got the money, she took it all in a lump sum."

"Like Horace. His dad signed everything over to him on his twenty-first birthday. The company. The estate. The money."

"Yes, like that, except Aunt Mary didn't get a house or company. She took my mom and ran away, changed their names and picked a small town to live in."

"How did they choose?"

"My mom says Aunt Mary took out a map of the United States, closed her eyes and put her finger down and that's how they ended up here."

"Isn't your Aunt Mary afraid her parents will see her TV show and find her?"

"I don't think so. Aunt Mary is fifty-five. What could they do?"

"That's true, I didn't think of that." She laughed.

We stopped to take a sip of our water as the trail looped around toward a steep hill.

"This is the last half mile," I said.

"Hello," a man's voice said from behind us.

Dexter's voice.

"So this is where you are hiking with a friend. Hi, Gabrielle," he said catching up with us.

"Hi," Gabrielle said, pulling at her sleeve. I'd noticed that as the hike progressed, I'd pulled up my sleeves and she'd done the opposite, constantly adjusting the thumb holsters.

"Hi, we're kind of in a hurry," she said.

"Oh, that's all right, I can walk fast." He fell in step with us. I glanced at Gabrielle's face and my empathy clicked in. It was possible that she was more panicked than I was at my time ticking away.

"Yeah, Gabrielle's estate is on the show Sell It Or Stay and she needs to get back to the set," I explained and took off at a slow jog.

"Here I was thinking I'd moved to a sleepy small town," he said, keeping pace with me. Gabrielle joined us in the jog.

We reached the parking lot and I could feel the

energy draining from my body, like the sand in a nearly empty hourglass. My time was running out. Anxiety zinged through my chest like a lightning bolt.

"Well, nice seeing you," I squeaked and opened the passenger door of Gabrielle's SUV, throwing my backpack in and slamming the door.

"Yeah, gotta run," Gabrielle said as she did the same, followed by pushing the start button and punching the SUV into reverse.

Dexter stood alone in the parking lot looking confused. I waved and smiled my best apologetic smile. He smiled back, raised a hand and turned back toward the trail we had just finished.

Had he figured out where I was hiking today and purposely planned to run into me? Why?

"Sorry, I don't like cops," Gabrielle said. "Let's just say my family doesn't have the best history with them."

As if I didn't know. But it wasn't my nature to dredge up the past. Honestly, I could barely handle digging into my own past to figure out why I was the way I was. So I was perfectly happy to sit here and pretend with Gabrielle, even though I knew her fear of the police had more to do with the present bruises she was hiding under her long sleeves than the past.

"That was fun," I said, changing the subject. I chugged my water, trying to swallow the anxiety.

"The anxiety is back?" Gabrielle asked.

"How did you know?" I asked.

"Well, your timer went off ten minutes ago," she explained.

"Oh," I said.

"Edgar told me to set a timer and get you back home

before it went off," she said. "Plus I'm feeling it too. Memories you know." As if her statement explained everything.

As upset as I should be at Edgar sharing about my issues, I wasn't. For a rare moment, I was more concerned about Gabrielle. Add to that, why was Dexter following me?

On the short drive back to The Cozy Corner Bookstore, both Gabrielle and my phone buzzed at the same time.

At this point, I had the urge to jump out of the car to escape the anxious feeling which had turned my bones and innards to jelly. My legs needed something solid like the bricks of my building, the feel of the hardwood floor under my feet. I grounded my feet by pushing them into the floorboard.

"I'm sorry," Gabrielle said. "I kept you out too long."

"Sure," I croaked, making no sense whatsoever.

My hands groped for something solid to hold onto. Gabrielle reached down into the console and pulled out one of my books, *Espresso Espionage at Evergreen Books,* and shoved it in my hands. "Read," she commanded.

I blinked and opened it to page one.

"Ashford was a sleepy town. Nothing ever happened here. Until today when ..." I faltered, sucking in shuddered breath.

"Keep reading," Gabrielle shouted.

I did. I read three paragraphs, my voice getting stronger with each word, my bones solidified once again. The seat beneath me grounded me as much as the words turned me back into a solid form instead of a hot mess of jelly about to melt off the face of the earth.

"You did it," she said. "We're here." Gabrielle clicked the button, turning off the car. "Let's get you inside."

Before I could refuse, she had jumped out of the car and opened my door, pulling me out, grabbing my backpack and guiding me inside as if I were a toddler going to story hour. "I have your backpack, your drink, and your jacket."

The next five minutes blurred in a flurry of hellos from customers and I vaguely remember running up the stairs to my apartment. Once inside, I collapsed on the couch and, by the force of pure will, I commanded my body to calm while I engaged in four sets of box breathing.

"Here you go," Gabrielle said as she gently placed a mug of coffee in my hands. "Holding something warm helps me."

For the first time since we left Christmas Tree Forest, I looked her full in the face. "Thank you," I said. "Wait, why are you crying?"

"I messed up. I always mess everything up," she said, wiping a tear from her perfect porcelain skin.

"Pretty sure that is my job description," I said. "I mean look at me. Strong female business owner and author who can't leave her apartment. What a joke."

I sipped my coffee. "What did you say about me? Everyone knows about my little problem?" I let the cool stableness of the couch and the familiar feel calm me.

"I shouldn't have said that," she said, gingerly lowering down beside me. "Oh… Edgar."

"What about Edgar?"

"I told him I'd give him a full report," she said as she stood and dusted imaginary dirt off her hiking pants. "He is going to be angry. I didn't follow the instructions to the tee."

"Listen Gabrielle, everyone is not angry with you all the time."

"Are you?"

"You mean right now? No, I'm grateful. You helped me go out and hike and have a great time."

Before Gabrielle could reply, Sage burst through the door. "Don't you two ever answer your phones?"

"What's going on?" I said. The truth was there was absolutely no reception at Christmas Tree Forest. And in our defense, we'd only gotten one notification in the Highlander on the way home while I was trying not to get sucked off the planet into the deep darkness of a panic attack.

"Horace is dead. Murdered," Sage blurted out.

CHAPTER 5
THE COZY CORNER'S MURDER SUSPECT

GABRIELLE CRUMPLED like the cinnamon coffee cake topping Bea made. Sage reached out to catch her and break her fall, but didn't get there in time. Gabrielle nicked her head on the edge of the walnut table. Blood spurted from her forehead, a mahogany circle pooling on the dark hardwood.

"Call 911," I yelled as I leaped from my position on the sofa and grabbed a dish towel from the kitchen.

"Did you tell her?" Edgar's deep, calming voice said from the doorway.

"No, I...." Sage didn't finish. Instead, her phone blared, "911, what's your emergency?"

Sage filled in the 911 operator as Edgar joined me in tending to Gabrielle, who was now on her knees.

Edgar lowered his lean, lanky frame to the floor and said, "Don't try to get up, I've got you."

"I'm sorry, Horace. I won't do it again. I promise. I know I embarrassed you." Then she looked down at her clothes with the polka dots of blood stretching and growing, eating up her soft spruce trekking pants, like a Christmas tree with deep red bulbs. "I'll change right now."

"Gabrielle, it's me Harper, you hit your head. You're in my apartment."

"Horace is going to be so angry. Don't tell him," she begged.

"Horace is dead," Sage said. Why was she doing this? Torturing Gabrielle. She had been my best friend my whole life, and this wasn't like her.

"Sage," Edgar said from his pretzel position on the floor. "You need to leave."

"Aren't you going to tell her?" Sage screamed. "Aunt Mary–"

Edgar interrupted her. "Not now Sage. Go downstairs and tell the paramedics where to come. Go! Now!"

Sage's willowy frame paused in the doorway, grief and sorrow etched in her face.

"No hospital," Gabrielle said before she passed out.

Minutes later, the paramedics marched up the stairs and took over. I watched out the front window of my office where I wrote my mysteries and prayed for a second time that my new-old friend would be okay.

"We need to talk," Edgar said.

"What's going on with Sage?" I asked.

"I'm sure she told you Horace was murdered."

"Yes, the news made Gabrielle fall and hit her head on the coffee table," I said, sinking into my office chair. My heart pounded in my chest, the weight of the situation pressing down on me.

"Authorities took your Aunt Mary into custody for the murder."

"Oh," I said, spinning my chair around to face the window again. My world spun out of control. The room felt like it was closing in, my breaths coming in shallow gasps. "Tell me what to do, Edgar. I don't know what to do. Where is Sage? I need her here." My voice wavered, desperation seeping into every word.

"I'm here," Sage said from the hallway outside my office. "I'm sorry Gabrielle hit her head. I wasn't thinking. I just wanted to tell you about Aunt Mary."

"Come in," Edgar said. "You didn't go downstairs did you?"

"No, I texted Zoe and told her to direct the paramedics." Sage had left her hiding place in the hallway and now stood in the middle of my office.

"What do we do, Edgar?" I repeated myself.

"You write mysteries, right? Now it's time to solve one. Do you think your aunt killed Horace?" Edgar said, standing to his full height and looking down at his blood-stained hands.

With the casualness of an after-dinner stroll, he walked to the coffee bar sink, squirted some soap on his hands, turned on the faucet, and washed his hands. I watched as the water turned from crimson to pink and finally clear.

"But I can't leave the building. I used more than my time today. My body is so dysregulated, I think I might pass out," I said, folding myself over like a pocket knife closing.

"Well, don't. Our Aunt Mary needs you," Sage said. "I need you."

"How can I help?"

"Well, how do you plot your novels?" Edgar asked, as if we were discussing a novel, not an actual murder.

"First, I use a giant whiteboard." I pointed to one tucked away in the corner of my office.

"Pull that out, Sage," Edgar ordered while he dried his hands on a paper towel.

She complied.

Edgar threw the paper towel in a small silver wastebasket beside the coffee bar sink before joining me next to my desk. I could feel the weight of his presence, a silent reminder of the gravity of our situation. My mind was still reeling from the news about Aunt Mary, and my agoraphobia was making it hard to breathe. I tried to focus on the task at hand, but a part of me just wanted to hide away.

"Now we have a murder board. Can you print out some pictures of the suspects?" Edgar's voice cut through my swirling thoughts.

"Me?" Sage said, her voice tinged with surprise.

"You've been on set taking photos and videos of everything, right?" Edgar asked, his tone calm.

"Oh! I have photos of the murder scene," Sage said, excitement creeping into her voice. "I was called on set today to get a few shots for social media. The landscaper found Horace's body and yelled for help. So I slipped back to the conservatory grounds. I had my camera. So naturally. Yes. Who are the suspects?"

"So far your Aunt Mary. Gabrielle...." Edgar paused, and I jumped in, the words spilling out of me before I could stop them.

"Gabrielle was hiking with me," I said, my voice

shaking slightly. I needed to protect Gabrielle, just as much as I needed to clear Aunt Mary's name.

"The murder happened this morning," Sage said, flipping her blonde bang out of her eyes. "We need a timeline."

"What? Where? How?" I asked, my mind racing. How had everything gone so wrong so quickly?

As they discussed the details, I felt a knot of fear and determination forming in my chest. Aunt Mary had raised me, had been there for me through everything. I couldn't let her face this alone. My agoraphobia threatened to hold me back, but I knew I had to push through it. For her.

I have to do this, I thought. If I don't, who will?

Despite my fears, a resolve took shape. I would solve Horace's murder. I would find the truth. My hands might have been shaking, and my heart might have been pounding, but I would not let Aunt Mary down. She needed me, and I needed to prove her innocence. This was my fight now.

"Now you're thinking," Edgar said, clapping his hands together. "I think his body was found this morning face down near the conservatory, hit in the head with a shovel or some sort of garden tool, I think."

"This sounds like something out of a game of Clue," Sage said. "Except for Aunt Mary being the prime suspect," She ran her hand through her pixie cut.

Sage motioned for me to give up my chair and sat

down to plug her memory card into the computer. "Should I print pictures of everyone on set?"

"Yes, you're right, Sage. This is like the game of Clue. Everyone is a suspect. Put them all up there and then we will eliminate people who we think have no motive," I said, finally warming up. "I'll just pretend this is one of my novels, not my Aunt Mary potentially spending the rest of her days in a prison cell."

After Sage printed the photos, we moved the murder board downstairs to the main area of my apartment so we'd have more room to work. My office was getting a little crowded with Rory thumping everyone in the shins with his tail. Sage tripped over him twice and Edgar had his own near miss, dodging Rory's body as he took a giant step over him, knocking into the murder board.

"I'll work on creating some behavior profiles," Edgar said, pulling a laptop out of a shoulder bag he'd left on the island when he came in earlier.

Half an hour later, we had twenty photos on the board. We worked our way through the people we thought had no motive, which turned out to be more difficult than we thought. Turns out, Horace had been rude and mouthy with everyone from the contractor to the caterer. Zoe had loads of videos, which she screencast to my TV, of Horace spitting mad and occasionally came near to punching, pushing, hitting or with his uncle Eustace, pushing him in the pool. Not to mention the altercation with my aunt in which he threw his phone into the pool.

"I'm going to go visit your Aunt Mary. You two stay here and keep working," he said. "We need to let her know we are doing something and she's not alone."

My phone buzzed, and I answered. "There's a detective down here and he wants to ask you a few questions," Zoe said in a breathless, frightened voice. "I told your aunt to fix her image, didn't I? You wouldn't believe what they're saying about her on social media. I tried, I really did."

I couldn't believe I was saying this, but it needed to be said. "Pull yourself together, Zoe. I'll be right down." What a hypocrite I was. I'm hiding in my apartment and Zoe is downstairs facing the public.

"Don't leave yet, please, Edgar. There's a detective here who wants to question me. I'd like you to be with me." I was pretty one hundred percent sure it was Detective Dexter.

Five minutes later, I was seated at a round table on the second floor of the bookstore, away from prying eyes. Zoe served Edgar, Detective Dexter, and me coffee and cookies before going back downstairs.

Before Dexter opened his mouth, I said, "You weren't on the hiking trail to see me. You were there to question Gabrielle."

"Woah, I guess working a murder investigation around a mystery writer is going to keep me on my toes."

Was he complimenting me or poking me with a rude jibe? Either way, the only thing that mattered at this point was proving Aunt Mary didn't murder Horace. In order to prove that, I needed to find out who did.

"What do you know so far?" I asked, gripping my coffee so hard I thought it would crack and shatter like my soul was right now. Every time I had needed some-one, Aunt Mary had been there. Every time. And the one time she had needed me, I had faced my fears and gone hiking with a potential murderer. Oh, Gabrielle, could it be you? Did you befriend me so I could be your alibi? No more facing my fears with fun outings. My daily hour and a half would be focused on solving Horace's murder.

"I'm asking the questions here." Just then a gaggle of teens carrying stacks of graphic novels and balancing coffees and sweets swept past us, parking on the couches beside us. They chatted loudly, nerding out on the artwork of the latest release.

"I really enjoyed…"one teen said, smacking his sugar-laden drink down with too much force, causing it to slosh out and onto the leather sofa.

"Gosh, Harper, I'm sorry!" he yelled, sopping it up with a napkin at the same time.

"Can't you tell them to be quiet?" Dexter asked.

"This isn't a library," I whispered. "It's fine, Liam. Good to see you. What do you think of the new graphic novel?"

"The graphics are amazing," he said, holding up the graphic novel for me to see.

"You're right," I said.

"Maybe we should do this down at the station," Dexter said.

"No," I said. "I'm out of time for today." Then I wished I could retract those words. I sounded like a freak. And what niece wouldn't want to go down to the station and do whatever she could to help her aunt who raised her, putting her career on hold to homeschool her?

"You look fully staffed," Dexter said, looking around and pushing his glasses up on his nose at the same time. "But I've never run a bookstore before, so maybe after you close?"

"Yes, why don't you come back later?" Edgar said. "Harper may need to attend to these customers," he jerked his head towards the teens. "I'll follow you down to the station so I can see Mary." Edgar stood and grabbed his bag.

Dexter followed suit. "Okay, I'll come by later, Harper." He grabbed two empty mugs.

"I'll get those," I said.

"Woah, dude, look at this!" a teen yelled.

Thank you, loud teens and Edgar for rescuing me. The thought of being stuffed in the back of a police car, or any car at this moment, felt suffocating. I sucked in a deep breath to make sure my lungs hadn't turned to jelly. Edgar had told me that imagining something was occurring produced the same bodily reactions as it actually happening. Breathe. Think about something else.

"Harper, you've gotta see this," Liam yelled.

I left the coffee cups and joined the teens, regulars who hosted a graphic novel club I mildly supervised. With everything going on, I'd forgotten it was on the schedule. My role was to listen, learn, and serve as the adult, which amused me since these graphic novel-loving teens had genius IQs and were often seen as misfits in town.

These "nerds" or "geeks" were the intelligent ones. If they could survive high school with a supportive community, they would be successful. When Liam Reed asked if their club could meet here instead of the high school, I readily agreed. This building could be their safe haven from bullies and name-calling, a place to quote graphic novels and drink coffee with sweets.

The teens' chatter and the sloshed coffee proved the club was a success.

I texted Zoe to let her know I was with the Graphic Gurus. Before I sat down with them, I grabbed a towel from the mini sink in the corner and cleaned up the rest of the coffee mess.

"Show me the new graphic novel," I said, plopping down next to Liam, grateful for the distraction.

I spend the next half an hour listening to the Graphic Gurus and laughing at their jokes and dry wit. Internally, I knew another clock was ticking. The clock on the investigation. The clock on the wall of the cell that my aunt sat in. Did they have clocks in cells? Or was it a dark, damp pit with the added punitive weight of not knowing how long you'd been there?

Another half hour later found me cleaning up after the teens. A few of them stayed, helping me haul cups and plates to the dumbwaiter and sending them down to the cafe kitchen. Sage joined me. "I have all the photos up on the board," she whispered.

"I'll be right up," I said.

"I'm going down to grab some coffee," she said.

"Any chance you could grab us some sandwiches?" I asked.

"Done," she said. With that, she ran down the stairs. "I'll be back in fifteen with your regular order," she yelled, her voice echoing off the brick.

Once back in my apartment, I studied the murder board and mentally eliminated suspects. I didn't physically remove them. I wanted Edgar and Sage to be here and agree before I removed any photos.

I couldn't imagine the caterer murdering Horace. Sure, he was rude, but this was an opportunity for her to gain more business. The photos of her spreads on social media must be an added bonus.

The contractor worked with my aunt regularly. While he didn't care for fame and fortune, he seemed pretty level-headed. He paid attention to detail which made him a favorite of not only Aunt Mary, but Eustace, who was a stickler for detail on these historic homes. I put a check beside his photo, the caterer, Marion, and Aunt Mary.

Then I stared at Gabrielle, beautiful and perfect, but what was hiding underneath? Her reaction earlier, thinking Horace had hit her, apologizing for embarrassing him and imagining she was on the ground because he'd beat her. I thought of the time-line - when she'd first come in the Cozy Corner, the day Aunt Mary announced they'd be filming. Gabrielle's sudden interest in me, the book club, and wanting to do things with me. Had this all been an elaborate ruse so she could use me as a sympathetic friend and alibi while she murdered her abusive husband? I circled her. Before I dug deeper into her motivation, I needed to read Edgar's behavioral analysis of her.

As I tapped the board, reviewing the next suspect, Sage burst in. "I have food!"

I jumped. Sage plopped the takeout bag on the table.

"Come and eat. Zoe is walking Rory and she's going to lock up."

"What time is it?" I asked.

"Oh, sorry I was gone so long. It's eight p.m.," she said. "I ran into so many people. All of them asking about Aunt Mary. No one believes she could have murdered him."

She'd been gone an hour, and I'd been in the zone. Edgar was right. Solving a crime with a murder board was like plotting a novel. Except backwards. When I wrote a novel, I plotted the murder first and then built a backstory. This time I needed to find out the backstory. Why did someone murder Horace?

I joined Sage at the table. "It's okay, I was busy with the murder board." I unwrapped my bacon avocado burger from the foil and shoved it in my mouth. It was with that first savory bite that I realized I hadn't eaten since breakfast. I'd been too nervous about the hike. *Little did I know,* I thought, quoting the movie *Stranger Than Fiction* to myself, that the hike wasn't the most difficult event of my day.

"Knock, knock," Dexter said from the doorframe of my apartment.

"Sorry, I left the door open for Rory," Sage said.

"You can't go in there," Edgar said. "This is her private residence." He stepped around Dexter on his way inside.

"Yes, I know. I walked Harper home after closing the other evening," he said with a grin.

I could feel Sage and Edgar's eyes boring into my pomegranate pinked cheeks. I swallowed the mass of avocado and bacon in one lump and it lodged in my esophagus. I grabbed my San Pellegrino and prayed the fizzy water would dislodge it. Success.

"I see," said Edgar. "In that case, come in."

"Yes, do," Sage said, patting the chair beside her. "Tell us all about walking Harper home."

"I'm here on official police business, so that story will have to wait for another time," he said as his skin flushed pink. "It is warm in here."

"Let me take your coat," Sage said, sliding her lithe body out from under the table as if she were in a pilates sequence. She leaned over my shoulder. "We have some stuff to talk about later." She slid to the coat rack and hung Dexter's coat up.

Why in the world did Dexter say that? He hadn't walked me to the door of my apartment. He hadn't set foot in here. He'd only walked me back to the door of the bookstore because I'd lied through omission.

"Let's get started," Edgar said.

"I'd like to talk to Harper alone," Detective Dexter said. Gone was the blushing man, replaced by a detective getting a job done.

"Not going to –" Edgar's statement was interrupted by two simultaneous occurrences. Rory bounding in the room, barking, and Dexter discovering the murder board which we had moved to the living room earlier and placed on an easel.

"What is this?" he said, standing. With three long strides he was in front of it. "Are you trying to solve the murder? You're an author. This is real life."

For some reason, that last statement cut right through me and wounded me. On the one hand, I'd hidden from real life, but he didn't know that. On the other hand, I was pretty durn good at writing about murder. How dare he?

"Yes, this is real life. My aunt's life. She didn't murder Horace. I'm going to prove that. I'm also going to find the real murderer." I had moved from my seat at the table and now stood face to face.

"What did you need to ask me?" I added.

He pushed his glasses up the bridge of his nose and answered, "Where were you this morning between eight a.m. and ten a.m.?"

"Here. I had my hour and half out this afternoon hiking. You know that already because you followed me to the Christmas Tree Forest trail."

"Your hour and half out?" he asked.

I'd instantly regretted saying that as soon as it was out of my mouth. My linear logical brain just couldn't come up with anything but the truth when stressed. Or any time, for that matter.

"She means, she took time off of running the book-store, to go hiking," Sage offered, stepping between us.

"Well, okay," he said.

With that, he stomped to the coat rack and grabbed his gray wool peacoat and shoved his arms in the sleeves. "I'm solving this. Even if your aunt did it."

"We'll see," I said.

"Still on for coffee tomorrow to discuss your book?" he said, his detective persona morphing back into the kind, protective, let-me-walk-you-home persona I'd met the other day.

"Absolutely," I said with more gusto than I meant to use.

After he left, shutting the door behind him, I realized Edgar and Sage were both staring at me.

"You have some avocado on your chin," Sage said and reached out and wiped it away.

"This is definitely a good sign," Edgar said with a smile, referring to my interaction with Dexter and future date. I'm not sure why my date was important right now with my aunt sitting in a jail cell.

Edgar patted me on the back and chuckled before grabbing his coat off the rack. "This has been a long day. I'm going home. Your aunt is going to be released on bail in the morning. I'll pick her up and bring her here."

CHAPTER 6

THE COZY CORNER REVELATIONS

THE CLOCK FACE READ four a.m.. Instead of snuggling back under the weighted blanket, a new addition and gift from Edgar, I wrestled it off and slid my feet into my slippers. With everything on my mind about the case and Dexter, I couldn't sleep.

After a short trip to the bathroom, I clicked a pod into the Keurig and turned on my desktop computer.

I decided to write for a few hours before I re-examined the murder board. Poirot (Rory), slept peacefully in his large corner bed. He was used to me rising pre-dawn and plunking away on the keyboard. The street lamps glowed like tiny white golf balls in the morning fog. If anyone traveled at this hour on foot, or in a vehicle, it would be slow going until the sun burned off the fog.

While I had a real murder to solve, plotting this new novel proved a challenge. I had a sudden inspiration and pulled out my iPad and pen. I opened the pen and paper app and scribbled a new plot. The setting - one of the many places I visited while in Paris. My mom could help me with the art descriptions which would be central to the murder. It was time for Emma Hawthorne to finally leave her comfort zone, and someone besides a local to give her a new mystery to solve.

As usual, I lost track of time. I moved about pacing the office, then typing up the notes I'd scribbled on my iPad. The acts of the book were coming together nicely. Next up, a subplot. As I typed my last idea and chugged the last of my third cup of coffee, Rory barked.

Someone punched in the code to my apartment door.

"Let's not wake her up," Aunt Mary said.

"No, let's not. She's probably scared to death. Why did you have to murder that nice man?"

"Nice man? He was an odious creature and I didn't murder him."

"You can't get along with anyone, can you?" Mom's voice rose an octave. "You just go around murdering anyone who rubs you the wrong way."

"What are you talking about? I've never murdered anyone."

"What about Father?"

"What about Father?" Aunt Mary said. I assumed they were helping themselves to coffee. It sounded as if they were slamming mugs on the counter.

"Now you've done it, you've shattered her favorite mug. You can't control your emotions."

"I repeat, what do you mean I murdered Father?"

"Well, he had a heart attack and hit his head on his desk in his study. At least that's what you told the police. You were the only one with him. Then we packed up and ran away."

"We packed up and left because Father had been sexually molesting me since I was eight. I couldn't leave you. He would start on you. He didn't? Did he?"

Silence. I didn't dare breathe lest they heard me.

"He hit me, slapped me most of the time. But he always apologized and gave me such nice gifts," Mom said.

There was the sound of sweeping and the clinking of what I assumed was my favorite mug being dumped in the trash.

"He was an abusive manipulator. A narcissist. I had to get you away from him. You don't even recognize an abuser when he literally smacks you in the face."

"But he was dead, why couldn't we stay with Mommy?" My mother sounded as if she were five years-old, instead of fifty-two.

"Mother didn't care what father did as long as we wore the right clothes and said the right things. It was all about image for her. Just like Horace was with poor innocent Gabrielle," she said.

"So you did murder him."

"I didn't murder anyone," Aunt Mary yelled. "Father isn't dead."

"But the police…"

"Yes, he had a heart attack. Yes, he hit his head. But he recovered. In fact, he's still … wait, you could have found that out yourself by searching on the internet. And what about you?"

"What about me?"

"You're still running, all over the globe, trying to

escape. You abandoned your own daughter. I raised her. I think I'm the stable one. I chose this small town to settle down in and have a normal life. A stable life."

"I'm not trying to escape. I'm a strong, successful woman," she said as if she didn't believe it.

"Oh… he did molest…" The last few words were drowned out by Rory barking and running down the stairs.

I followed him down. When I breezed past them, grabbing Rory's leash, they froze.

"I'll be right back. Rory needs to go out."

I shoved my jacket over my pjs, stuffed my feet in rain boots and ran down the stairs after Rory, tears streaming down my cheeks. My aunt and mother had been through so much worse than I had. In fact, my childhood sounded perfect compared to theirs. Grandfather, whom I'd never met, sexually molested both of them. No wonder Aunt Mary had been drawn to Gabrielle and hated Horace, evidenced by the huge shift in her personality while working with him. Meanwhile, my mother hadn't abandoned me. Well, she had, but she'd been running from her father and rewriting the narrative, making Aunt Mary the villain.

I stumbled around in the fog. Rory took no notice of it, pulling me along to the park.

"Hey, you're out early," Dexter's voice said from the fog.

"So are you," I managed.

"Yeah, out for a quick jog, but it's not working." He stepped from the blue spruces at the park, as if he was in a scene from *The Lord of The Rings*, except he was wearing running shorts and a tee.

"I can't see five feet in front of me."

"Yes, the fog here is brutal, but Rory doesn't seem slowed down by it," I answered.

"Pajamas, huh? Nice look. Is this part of your hour and a half out," he said jokingly.

I let Rory off the lead and he leaped into the fog, growling at a squirrel who barked back. "No, walking Rory… you're kidding, right?"

"Of course, I'm sure the Cozy Corner isn't even open yet, so you can take as much time as you like."

If he only knew…

"Hey, have you been crying?" he said, looking me full in the face.

"Yes, it's all this going on with my aunt."

I didn't go into detail of what I'd just learned about Aunt Mary and my mother. Rory was already back from his squirrel hunt, rubbing up against my coat, ready to head home.

"See you later for our coffee date?" he called after me as Rory and I were swallowed by the fog.

"Yes," I yelled back.

It was as if Rory sensed his morning walk needed to be shortened since Ben had left. Ben let Rory take his time. Rory had a keen feel when something was too much for me. He was correct. I didn't want to go back to my apartment and face the two most important females in my life.

After punching in the code and stepping inside the bookstore, I wiped Rory's feet and let him off the leash. He followed me up the stairs wagging his tail in antici-pation of breakfast. My stomach growled.

Mom and Aunt Mary hadn't left my apartment. As I

removed my outerwear, I noticed mom was studying the murder board. Aunt Mary stood beside the counter and the waffle iron beeped signaling it was ready for batter. She used a Pampered Chef muffin scoop and filled all four molds.

"You must be hungry," she said. "I made fresh coffee." As if the conversation I'd overheard hadn't taken place.

Once I'd wiggled out of my crock rain boots, I thanked her, kissed her on the cheek, and joined Mom at the murder board.

"What is this?" Mom asked while giving me a quick side hug.

"It's a murder board."

"A what?"

"You heard me, I'm going to solve Horace's murder. That's the only way to prove Aunt Mary didn't do it."

"I don't think that's a good idea," Mom said, pursing her lips. "You should let the authorities handle it."

I filtered her statements through the fresh lens (fresh to me) of my mom's behavioral patterns. Spending time with Edgar taught me never to accept people's reactions at face value. For some reason, Mom thought Aunt Mary had taken her from her family and there was no Liam Neeson-dad coming to rescue her so she continued to run across the globe. She not only didn't view Aunt Mary as her rescuer from her sexually molesting, narcissist father, she hadn't realized that Aunt Mary had rescued me as well.

"Mom," I said. "I'm doing this. Aunt Mary has done everything for me. It's time I helped her in whatever way I can. I'm good at creating murders. I'm going to use my skill and solve this one." With that, I swung the murder board around so that the empty side was visible.

"Breakfast," Aunt Mary said.

CHAPTER 7

TEXTING THE TRUTH AT THE COZY CORNER

AN HOUR LATER, I joined my new bookkeeper, Rosy, in the Cozy Corner office. Because of my coffee date later with Dexter, I'd taken extra care to choose my dress today, a mustard yellow with blue swirls like Vincent Van Gogh's *Starry Night* in reverse. I added to the dress a mustard colored cardigan and chocolate brown lace up boots. My blonde curls seemed a little excited today as well, meaning I couldn't get them to calm down.

My normal protocol for the day was to throw on a dress and boots, put my hair in a bun if it didn't cooperate and walk down the stairs to the bookstore. Today, I asked Mom to help me with a little makeup which snapped her out of her funk. She opened her purse and within ten minutes, she'd applied a tasteful amount, giving me the *natural* look with a touch of pink on my lips.

"Only emphasize one part of your face at a time," she said.

I gazed in the round mirror above the sectional, approving of her work. "Why my lips?"

"Your big baby blue eyes don't need any help. A bit of mascara does the trick." She eyed my dress. "How about a more fitted sophisticated dress?"

I glanced down at my dress. "I love this dress."

"Darling, while I appreciate the ode to Van Gogh, you're not a painting. You're a lovely young woman with a figure somewhere under there." She tugged at the skirt of my boho dress, her lips pursed in disapproval.

"There's not going to be any filming today," she continued her tone carrying an undertone of impatience.

"What?" I blinked, my heart sinking. My hands instinctively went to my dress, smoothing it down self-consciously. Frustration bubbled up inside of me.

She crossed her arms, tilting her head slightly and a misused yet slightly condescending smile played on her lips. "I assumed you wanted to be camera ready."

I sighed, feeling tears prick at the corners of my eyes I ran a hand through my hair, trying to keep my voice steady. "No, I just want to look my best today."

Thankfully, my mother accepted the excuse and didn't pry. I couldn't say "I'm enamored with the new detective. His sweaters and corduroys make me swoon." Dexter looked as if he'd just stepped out of prep school instead of a police station. He had a habit of pushing his glasses up on his nose, which I loved for some strange reason. I'm sure my mother would love to give him some fashion advice as well, such as wear a suit and a tie, and get some contacts.

As angry as I was at his challenging me last night and pretty much telling me to stick to writing about murders instead of solving one, I was still looking forward to our coffee date. He wanted to discuss my book. I planned on using the opportunity to prove I *could* and *would* solve Horace's murder.

Aunt Mary went home to shower and rest up from her night in jail, which she spent alone, thankfully. Nothing like those murder shows with the scenes of cells full of drunks and derelicts. Of course, Evergreen Heights is a small town, so the percentage of drunks and derelicts is smaller due to the population size alone.

I soared through the morning activities, the Cozy Corner Bookstore buzzing with energy. Bea delivered the baked goods personally.

"I wanted to check on you. How are you doing? I heard your aunt is out on bail. How could anyone believe she did this?" she said as she placed iced cinnamon rolls in display cases. Bea didn't give me an opportunity to answer. Instead she talked while she unpacked and loaded the rest of the baked goods in display cases.

"I'm so glad you're doing well," she said as she gave me a quick hug, grabbed her boxes and scurried to the door and across the street to her bakery.

"How does she know how you are doing?" Zoe asked. "She didn't look at you or let you get a word in edgewise."

I didn't have the opportunity to answer as Clare and Ashley showed up early for story time.

"We're here to help," Clare said.

"What do you need?" Ashley asked, scanning the

store with wide eyes, as if the murderer may be lurking behind the bookshelves. "Crazy to think we've got a murderer right here in our small town."

Clare said, "I know. Ben left his big city corporate job when I was pregnant with Theo and we moved here so we could raise the kids in a safe small town."

"Oh, I forgot. I assembled a craft for the kids. Figured you had a lot on your mind," Ashley said. "It's a tad messy and we need water. Where should I set it up?"

I loved the moms of Evergreen Heights. Despite their limited hours of sleep and time to do anything for themselves, they volunteered to help all the time, not just at the bookstore, but everywhere.

"There's a sink on the second floor. Maybe you can set it up while I read to the first group?" I said. "Could you tell me what it is so I can pick a book to match?"

"It's grass eggheads. You take an egg shell, dry it out. Poke out the top and add soil, grass seed, and finish it off with a face. In a few days he'll sprout hair. In a few weeks, the kids can give him a hair cut," she laughed. "Don't worry. I hollowed three dozen eggs."

I grinned. "Someone ate a huge omelet."

"Don't be silly, I've been saving egg shells. So has Clare and a few other moms in our neighborhood." Ashley added, while holding up a satchel with egg cartons in it as proof.

"Thank you so much, I'll go find a book if you want to go set everything up."

Babies Audrey and Peregrine snoozed in their carseats while Theo and Dominic drank hot chocolate at the counter, filling Zoe in on their morning. I overheard the word "mu-duh" come out of Theo's mouth. I prayed he was parroting a conversation and didn't actually know what it meant.

I chose *Play With Me* by Marie Hallets, a Caldecott Honor book about a little girl asking animals to play with her. She approached a grasshopper, frog, turtle and other woodland creatures with this request "Will you play with me?" The book seemed appropriate for the spring season and the craft.

The book and the craft were a huge success with all three story hours. After each story hour, the kids ran around asking each other "Will you play with me?" and then plopping on the floor while waiting for the animals to join them.

The grass egghead craft was a hit, too. Sure we made a huge mess, but the kids had a blast. Each left cradling their egg, which was carefully wrapped in bubble wrap to protect it.

The kids had learned two important lessons that day - to sit still and wait, which we practiced like the little girl in *Play With Me*, and how to hold an object gently. A few kids cracked their eggs and tears followed, but we had enough spares to make sure every child left with an egghead, thanks to Ashley. To ensure we didn't run out, I had Bea on alert to save egg shells.

Ashley and Clare were troopers, helping through all three story hours. As they packed up and I finished cleaning up, Ashley said, "We're going across the street for brunch before we take the kids home for a nap. Why don't you join us?"

"Ash, she doesn't leave the building," Clare whispered while swinging her diaper bag/purse towards her.

Ashley leaned to the side and missed the swinging diaper bag. "Sure she does. She and Gabrielle went hiking yesterday."

"You did?" Clare asked.

"I did." I smiled. "Thanks for the invitation, but I have a new novel I'm working on that's begging me to sit down and write it!"

Ten minutes later, I was back in my apartment, whipping up a snack before I sat down to finish plotting my new novel, set in Paris and involving an art theft as well as a murder.

I'd almost forgotten about the real murder. Almost. But there it was calling me from the murder board in my living room.

I pulled out my phone and texted Gabrielle. Whether she'd befriended me to cover the murder of her husband or not, I should at least check on her. That was the right thing to do.

I texted:

Hey, how are you?

I'm fine. Thanks for checking on me. My husband is dead.

I know. I'm sorry.

I'm afraid they think I did it.

What?

Was my Aunt Mary in the clear? Just like that? I didn't think murder investigations jumped from one main suspect to another that quickly.

I haven't been arrested. It's just a feeling. I need to tell you something.

Yes?

Was she going to confess to the murder in a text message?

Gabrielle replied:

I really need to talk to you in person.

I answered:

I'm in my apartment until "The Classics" arrive at 10:00.

Her final text read:

Be there in half an hour.

CHAPTER 8
THE COZY CORNER'S MURDER BOARD

TRUE TO HER WORD, Gabrielle showed up half an hour later, sporting a butter yellow blazer and trousers. She hesitated in the doorway of my apartment after I opened the door.

"You're going to be shocked when I tell you this," she said.

"Come in and I'll make us some coffee here so we can talk privately," I replied.

I busied myself in the kitchen, loading up the French Press, turning on the burner below the tea pot, and rummaging in the fridge for something to serve. I found a few cinnamon rolls.

Having some coffee and cinnamon rolls on hand saved me from going downstairs and answering questions from customers and their pitying glances. What did Gabrielle need to confess? She murdered her husband. In that case, I had chosen the not-lesser of two evils. I'd locked myself in my apartment with a murderer.

"Is this what I think it is?" I peeked into the living room to see what she was referring to. Gabrielle stood next to the murder board, examining it.

Since we were being honest with each other now, I laid it all out there. "It's a murder board. I'm going to solve Horace's murder."

The tea kettle screamed, causing both of us to jump.

As I poured the water in the French Press, she gasped."My photo is on the board. Do you think I did it?"

I arranged two cinnamon rolls in a covered dish and placed them in the microwave to warm them. "Is that what you came to tell me?" As I spoke, I moved closer to the kitchen knives.

Gabrielle said nothing. She moved to the sectional, sat down and put her face in her hands.

"Is it wrong that I'm glad he's dead?" she wept.

I wasn't sure if I should leave the safety of the knives to comfort her. The microwave beeped and I busied myself with putting the cinnamon rolls on dessert plates and grabbing napkins. With nothing else to do except wait for the coffee to finish in the press, I joined her in the living room.

She raised her head as I set a plate in front of her.

"I'm a horrible person. I was horrible to you all those years ago and I'm a worthless piece of crap that Horace rescued from the gutter."

"Who said you were a worthless piece of crap?" I asked, mimicking her words, hoping she'd continue and confess if she did it. If she tried to overpower me, I could smear a cinnamon roll in her face. That wouldn't work, but I couldn't think straight.

"Horace said it. *Every day*. Eustace has been so kind and helpful. He came to the hospital last night and sat with me." She wiped her eyes with the napkin.

"What did you need to tell me in person, Gabrielle?"

"I need to show you. It's shocking, so brace yourself." She stood and pulled at the sleeve of her blazer and let it slip to the floor. Underneath she wore a sleeveless off-white silk blouse. Her arms bore multiple bruises of different hues. Some dark brown as if they were old. Some fresh, purple and blue.

"Only Eustace knows. This is why I didn't want to go to the hospital yesterday. Horace said if I told anyone, he would kill me."

"Horace did this to you?" I said.

She fell back on the sofa and grasped her head in both hands. "Yes, since our wedding day. Don't you see? I'm going to be accused of murder."

"Did you murder him?" I said, quickly backpedaling. "I mean, that's what the police are going to assume."

"I know. That's why I came to you. You write about murder. No one knows more about murder than you, except maybe the new detective who looks as if he stepped right out of an English boarding school," she said.

"He does," I laughed.

"No offense. That sounded horrible, no one knows about murder…"

The kitchen timer saved me from having to reply. I popped up, pressed the coffee, poured it and rejoined her. Instead of sitting down. I handed her a cup. "Join me at the murder board."

She grabbed her blazer and slipped it back on before joining me. Her hands clutched the coffee cup tightly, seeking warmth. "You don't seem shocked at my bruises," she remarked, her eyes fixed on the board.

"I knew," I admitted, glancing at her. "Edgar has been helping me find the right services to support you."

"Of course," she murmured, nodding slightly. "You'd figure it out." Suddenly, she squinted at the board. "Wait, why is Uncle Eustace up there?"

"Should I take his photo off?" I asked, watching her reaction carefully.

"Why would he kill his nephew? Plus, he was on my side. He didn't want to sell the family home," she replied, her voice tinged with frustration as she crossed her arms defensively.

"Gabrielle, I can't take him off the murder board just because he's been kind to you," I explained, shaking my head. "That's not how investigations work."

She sighed, her shoulders slumping. "I guess that means I'm staying up there too."

"Yes," I confirmed, meeting her gaze. "And be prepared for the police to question you. Be honest," I advised, offering a reassuring smile.

For the next fifteen minutes, we talked about every photo on the murder board. She filled me in a bit more on the family history. I filled her in on the arguments Eustace and Horace had recently. I pulled my phone out of my dress pocket and showed her the video of Horace pushing Eustace in the pool. And for full disclosure, the video of Aunt Mary arguing with Horace.

I looked at my watch. "Oh, The Classics will be here in a minute. I have to go back downstairs."

She reached her manicured hand and wiped a tear from her face. "Thank you. This past month spending time with you, is the first time in years I've felt as if I could have a few thoughts of my own."

With that, we set our mugs on the coffee table and hurried downstairs. Halfway down the stairs we met Sage coming up.

"Oh, hi," she said. "Harper, could I speak to you privately for a moment?"

Gabrielle took the hint and left us standing in the stairwell.

"You're talking to the murderer?" Sage declared her face an inch from mine.

I backed up one stair. "You don't know that. Besides, how else am I going to question everyone?"

She stepped back, tensing her shoulders. "You don't do it alone. You have me there. Or Edgar. Or that Poindexter detective."

I leaned against the cold stairwell wall. "She wanted to tell me that Horace had been physically and verbally abusive. She said she was glad he was dead."

Sage paused mid-step, turning to face me with a look of disbelief. "Harper, you're so gullible," her tone laced with exasperation as she crossed her arms, her brow furrowing.

I straightened up, bristling at the comment. "What do you mean by that?"

"Well, a little over a month ago, Gabrielle didn't give you the time of day. She shows up, buys your books, joins your book club, acts like your friend..." She looked down the stairs and let out an exasperated huff. Her face puffed up like a tomato about to explode out of its skin. "You …." She turned and stormed down the stairs.

I followed and grabbed her by the elbow. "You don't think I haven't thought of those things?"

She relaxed her shoulders, her face following suit. "You just invited a murderer to your apartment. I'm just concerned about you."

She hugged me. "Be careful. Don't interview anyone else without Edgar or me. Or the detective."

I promised not to. I joined The Classics. The topic of conversation, of course, was the murder. The bookstore buzzed with more customers than usual.

Some hoped to get a glance of Aunt Mary, or just get the latest scoop, evidenced by their questions. "Is your Aunt Mary here? Is Sage covering the story for the paper?"

There were others who were genuinely concerned and offered hugs and kind words.

Secretly, I hoped Aunt Mary wouldn't show up today and that my mother would go do something artsy.

I made it through the next three hours and ate a quick bite before my coffee date with Dexter to discuss *Cappuccino Chaos at Cozy Corner.* I reapplied the light pink lipstick after brushing my teeth. Then I grabbed a table on the second floor and waited.

"They said I could find you here," Eustace straightened his bow tie and lowered himself into the chair beside me.

"Oh hello," I said. Both hoping he would leave and that he would stay and answer some questions. Then I remembered I'd promised Sage I wouldn't question any suspects alone. But he wasn't really a suspect, I told myself. It was fine. I'm sure Dexter would arrive any second.

"Gabrielle told me she came and spoke to you this morning." He smiled.

"Yes," I said.

"I'm heartbroken," he said. "I've lost my nephew and found out he was abusing his wife all within twenty-four hours."

Eustace's expression turned sympathetic, though his eyes remained sharp. "Gabrielle's been through quite a lot. It's such a pity that these personal issues have impacted her so deeply. It's really not her fault, poor thing. I suppose we all have our burdens to bear."

"I'm so sorry," I said, patting him clumsily on the arm.

"Oh, sorry. I didn't come to pour out my troubles to you. You've got enough on your plate with your aunt being accused of murder." He paused. "I just stopped by to tell you, I'll make sure Gabrielle gets all the help she needs. I'll make sure the remodel is completed, with or without your aunt. Gabrielle can keep the house, like she wanted. I'll move in with her so she's not alone."

He leaned in slightly, lowering his voice as if sharing a confidential tidbit. "I think having someone there, especially someone who can provide a calm presence, might help her tremendously. It's such a crucial time for her, and I believe my being there might offer some stability."

Eustace made a show of adjusting his suit jacket. "If you ever need any assistance from the historical society, do let me know. We'd be more than happy to help. It's important to support each other, especially during trying times."

"That's sweet," I said, not knowing what else to say to the aunt-murdered-my-nephew comment. Something wasn't right. I couldn't put my finger on it.

Dexter's arrival ended our conversation. Eustace stood, straightened his tie, and said, "I'll be going. Don't worry about Gabrielle."

After he'd descended the stairs, Dexter and I exchanged hellos. "What was that all about?"

"Are you one of the murder suspects?" I asked quickly.

"No," he laughed.

I grabbed his hand. "Let's go upstairs to my apartment. I have so much to fill you in on."

CHAPTER 9

SENSORY OVERLOAD AT THE COZY CORNER

MY FACE TURNED fifty shades of embarrassed when I realized I'd just dragged Dexter into my apartment. He'd agreed to a coffee "meeting" to discuss my book.

After we were both inside my apartment and I'd gently closed the door, Dexter made himself at home. Leaning on the kitchen island he said, "I ordered some coffees for us. Do they deliver to your apartment?"

I straightened my back and pushed my shoulders back to look confident and in control. "I'll text Zoe. She can send someone up with them."

"I thought we were going to discuss your book *Cappuccino Chaos at Cozy Corner,*" he said playfully, and I realized the implications of inviting him into my home.

"Forget the book for now." I walked to the murder board. "I have so much to tell you."

He followed me to the murder board. It was evident in his body language that he had shifted into detective mode. "About the murder? The investigation? I thought we agreed you would let me handle the investigation and you would stick to writing books."

"No, you said that. I didn't agree," I replied as I texted Zoe:

Can you send someone to bring Dexter and my coffee order to my apartment?

Zoe:

Sure, boss! That's why you wore your Van Gogh dress. For your date. Heart emoji.

"You're out of your depth." He faced me, brows furrowed.

"Fine. I won't share what I've learned. You can take the long road and find the clues yourself."

"Yoohoo!" my mom's voice called from the other side of my apartment door. "I can't open the door."

Leaving Dexter standing in the middle of the room, I strode to the door and opened it. My mother stood there holding our coffees.

"Oh!" She smiled. "You moved the date to your apartment."

I turned on my heel, irritated at the interruption, and walked to the island. "Not a date, Mom. Dexter was just leaving."

Dexter had joined us at the island. He relieved my mom of the coffee.

She puckered her lips and pouted. "Oh, why?"

"He doesn't want my help with the case. He says I'm out of my 'depth'."

I grabbed my coffee and took a gulp.

"As much as I would hate for my daughter to put

herself in harm's way, sharing a few clues from the safety of her own home wouldn't hurt." She smiled.

I grabbed her by the arm and led her away from the island. "What are you doing here Mom?"

She glanced over her shoulder and smiled at Dexter. "You texted me and said you had a new book idea and needed help with art and Paris."

"Mom, I texted you that this morning."

"And I'm here now."

I knew my mother had come to spy on my coffee "meeting," not to share her knowledge of Parisian art.

"Besides, your Aunt Mary is sleeping. There's nothing happening on the set of Sell It Or Stay."

While she talked, she moved to the table, pulled out a chair, removed her coat, and plunked her purse on a bench, a sure sign she'd be staying for a while.

"By the way, I ordered some food from that fabulous bakery across the street and a carafe of coffee from downstairs. Zoe is sending one of your little minions to fetch everything for me. Shall we talk about the murder board?"

"Mom, my employees aren't minions and you can't order them around."

I glanced at Dexter who seemed to enjoy the interchange. I filtered Mom's sudden change in behavior through my new lens of behavioral patterns. After the confrontation with Aunt Mary this morning, Mom clicked into diva mode, the one she operated in most often. Was this a mask she wore to pretend she hadn't been abused and sexually molested? Was Aunt Mary right? Mom was still running? Instead of bringing up our messed up family history in front of Dexter who obviously wasn't leaving, I joined her at the table.

"Dexter, dear, why don't you grab the murder board and set it up in here. It wouldn't hurt to let Harper share what she's learned would it?"

She crossed her legs and leaned back in her chair.

Well, it would hurt, because half of what I planned to share happened to be about her and my aunt. I knew from reading murder mysteries, the worst approach for those accused of murder was to hide family secrets. That practice always came back to bite you.

Under Mom's spell, Dexter set his coffee down and complied. Ten seconds later, Mom and Dexter sat opposite each other at the table as I stood like a teacher at the whiteboard.

The fatigue and shock of the day washed over me. I suddenly felt dizzy. I reached for a chair, missed and fell on my bottom on the floor. As my kitchen spun in a kaleidoscope of orange, green, and white, I practiced a few sets of box breathing with my head between my legs.

"Are you okay, Harper?" Dexter asked, his hand heavy on my back. How and when he moved to the floor, I didn't know. "Should we call 911?"

"No, we don't need to. Harper is agoraphobic."

My mother said in a quick measured tone, as if she were embarrassed by me.

"I know," he said. "But we're inside."

He knew? How did he know?

She stood and moved away from me as if my panic were contagious.

"Let me call Edgar, he's her therapist. She has these

things called triggers. I think she's had too many today. You need to take your hand off her. That will make the panic attack worse."

First, thanks Mom for pouring out all my oddities in front of the first man I've ever been interested in before we've even had one date. Second, why don't you just have Sage come and take photos and run an article in the newspaper. Third, his hand felt comforting, not stifling.

"Okay," he said, not moving his hand. I had a horrible feeling that I said the third point out loud.

Mom was on the phone telling Edgar I'd had another episode. Before she finished, strong arms lifted me from the floor and carried me through the living room and deposited me on the couch. While my mother shouted at Edgar and ordered him to drop everything and come and take care of his patient, strong arms picked me up again.

"Where is your bedroom?"

"Upstairs," I whispered, my eyes clenched tightly shut. Like a child who doesn't want to listen to her mother, I had a strong urge to shove my fingers in my ears.

As Dexter set me on the bed he asked, "Is she always like this?"

"She's extra spicy today because her sister…" I didn't finish the sentence. I leaned back on my pillow.

He rummaged on my bedside table while Rory stuck his paws on the comforter and whimpered. I don't think Rory wanted to hear my mom yell either. "Do you have some noise-reducing headphones?"

"No," I whispered. I had the sensation of sinking

into the darkness. If I gave in, it would swallow me up and I'd disappear.

I struggled and fought as if I were fighting for my life.

"Don't fight it," Dexter said. "I'm putting your weighted blanket on you. Your body is telling you to rest."

"How do you know?" I rasped.

He tucked the weighted blanket around my arms. "That's a story for another time."

"Edgar isn't coming," Mom yelled as she stomped up the stairs. "The incompetence of some people."

Dexter met her at the top of the staircase. "I think we've got it under control. She's resting. Let's go downstairs."

For the next few minutes, I strained to make sense of their muffled conversation. With no success, I snuggled down under my weighted blanket and cried for my broken self. I realized I really liked Dexter, but how could it work? If we got married and had children, I could take them to the park for exactly an hour and a half. Wait, where did that come from? Marriage. I'd made a pact with myself when my Aunt deeded the building to me that I would live here alone until I died. Alone.

When I woke up, my apartment was dark and quiet. The stars twinkled from the picture window in my office, which was part of my bedroom. I struggled to free myself from the weighted blanket.

"You're awake," Edgar's voice said from the darkness. I turned my head to the direction of his voice. His dark complexion camouflaged him. The edges of his silver afro glowed, giving him the appearance of a ghost with no face.

"Oh," I said, my mouth sticky and heavy. "Did my mother order you here?" I croaked.

"Here, drink this." He handed me a water bottle and clicked on the lamp. "Yes, in the middle of a doctor's appointment. She called me incompetent."

"Sorry about that," I said, shifting beneath the covers and rubbing my eyes.

He stood by the bed, his concern evident as he looked down at me. "She's worried about you," he said, his voice soft.

I pushed myself up on the pillows, trying to clear the fog from my mind. "How long have I been asleep?" I asked, glancing around the room.

"Four hours," he answered, pulling up a chair and sitting beside the bed, his expression grave.

"Dexter? My mother?" I asked, my voice trembling slightly as I met his gaze.

"When I arrived your mother was filling Dexter in on your family's history, unfortunately, not painting your aunt in a very good light. She thinks your aunt murdered your grandfather. This isn't boding well for your aunt."

"I've got to get up and work on the investigation." I stumbled out of bed and over to my desk.

Edgar stood and steadied me with his hand under my forearm. "I'm sorry, I shouldn't have shared their conversation with you, yet. To answer your other question, Dexter went back to work. He promised to text you later."

I scanned the room for my phone which Edgar

produced from his blazer pocket. "I kept it downstairs while you slept. Don't worry, I didn't read any of the incoming texts."

I had twenty text messages. Five from my aunt. Five from my mother. One from my dad. Four from Sage. Three from Gabrielle. Two from Dexter.

He turned on his heel. "I'll let you read those. I'm going downstairs to warm up the dinner your aunt sent over."

"Wait," I said, patting the reading chair next to my desk. "Please tell me what happened. To my body."

"In simple terms," he explained, his voice gentle but clear, "your body needed rest from the triggers and sensory input. Since you struggle with recognizing your body's needs, it shut down. Like a computer. It needed a reboot."

He paused, allowing the information to sink in, his eyes never leaving mine. "How do you feel?" he asked.

"I feel as if my mouth is stuffed with cotton balls. My muscles feel like hot taffy. And oddly enough, I feel relaxed."

"Good. You feeling relaxed is a great sign. Drink your water. Stay off the computer."

He stood and moved towards the stairs. "Oh, before I forget, you received a gift. Here it is." He grabbed a box wrapped in yellow paper covered with blue swirls off my night stand and handed it to me. "Come downstairs when you're ready."

I spent the next ten minutes reading texts and simultaneously casting glances at the gift with the navy blue bow. I hadn't read the card yet and I didn't want to rip the beautiful paper.

Aunt Mary sent me five texts asking me if I was okay, whether I needed dinner, or if she should come over.

My Mom had sent me five texts, two about the incompetence of Edgar and my employees (who didn't seem keen on waiting on her hand and foot -my interpretation). Two asking if I needed her to send my aunt or a psychiatrist. One telling me she told dad to text me.

Dad:

Hope you are doing well. Mom said to text you.

Zoe sent four messages, one asking if I'd had a good date with Dexter. One saying my aunt had texted her saying I'd had an episode and was I okay. The other two, just checking on me.

Gabrielle sent me three, apologizing for hiding the truth from me. Another saying she heard my mother in the cafe telling everyone I'd had an episode and she was sorry if it were her fault. The third said she was being questioned by the police in the morning.

Dexter's texts said.

Hope you're feeling better.

Did you get the gift?

I sent quick texts to my mom, aunt, and Zoe letting them know I was okay. I ignored Gabrielle's and my dad's for now.

I picked up the package and gently opened it, trying not to rip the paper so I could save it.

The box stated:

Noise Reducing Headphones

I put them on and texted Dexter.

I'm fine. Thank you for checking on me. Thanks for the gift.

With the headphones on, I joined Edgar in the kitchen. "What are these for?" I asked.

I didn't hear the reply. He motioned for me to remove them. "To reduce the noise. The premise is when you're in sensory overload, to block one of the senses. I should have recommended them. Was that in the package?"

"Yes, from Dexter."

He whistled. "Expensive gift. Dinner is ready. Let's eat."

We chatted about books while we ate. I avoided the fact that I'd had a mental and physical breakdown five hours earlier.

After dinner, as Edgar loaded the dishwasher, he asked, "Would you like me to stay the night?" Exactly what a real father would say. My father took time out of his ultra busy schedule to text me because mom had told him to. Not because he was concerned about me.

"No, I think I'm fine. I'm going to watch some TV and go to bed," I said, sinking into the cushions of the couch and reaching for the remote on the coffee table.

He leaned against the counter, his eyes fixed on me with a concerned expression. "May I give you some advice?" he asked.

I looked up from the phone screen, raising an eyebrow. "Don't investigate?" I replied.

He shook his head, pushing off from the counter and stepping closer. "No, you're an intelligent woman. You see details others overlook." He paused, placing a hand on the back of the couch as he leaned in slightly. "My advice is don't try to do it all."

"I'm doing too much. That's your advice?" I was

shocked and happy at the same time. It wasn't "you're broken. You're horribly flawed. Just stay here in your building until your bones and brain rot away."

"Let me explain it in another way. Everyone has a trauma bucket. Your bucket is ¾ full so when you stress your body too much, it overflows. Like earlier."

"So how do I avoid that?" I asked.

"For now, I think you should get someone else to conduct story hour. Don't feel as if you have to join The Classics every day. You keep adding items to your metaphorical plate and not removing any."

"Oh," I said.

"You're not a machine, Harper. Your body needs time to recover from stress and too much sensory input."

"So don't do my hour and a half outing?" I felt as if I were backsliding in my recovery right before my eyes.

"No.You absolutely need to get out an hour and a half a day. You've built up to that. We don't want you to lose that," he said with a smile. "Just hand over some of your other responsibilities while you do this." He motioned toward the murder board.

"Use those," he added, pointing to my noise-reducing headphones.

He hugged me and left me in my clean kitchen. I moved to the sofa and clicked on the TV, opting for a streaming service with no commercials and no local news. With the murder mystery movie playing in the background, I stood and went to the murder board and scribbled clues. I didn't know how long I'd spent at the board before I heard a muffled banging. I hadn't real-ized I had slipped on my noise reducing headphones.

CHAPTER 10
THE COZY CORNER LATE NIGHT VISITOR

I SLIPPED OFF THE HEADPHONES, checked the time - ten p.m., and answered the door. No one could enter the building at this time of night without the code so it must be one of my employees.

I opened the door. "Eustace," I said. "How did you get in?" More importantly, why was Eustace visiting me?

"I'm so sorry," he said. "Your bookkeeper is working downstairs. I was taking a walk. I saw the light on and well, I wanted to check on you and apologize. Can I come in?" His gaze swept the apartment, landing on the murder board.

"No, I don't think that's a good idea." I pulled my robe tie tighter. "I'm getting ready for bed."

"I see," he said. "It's just that I need to talk to you for a minute. It's important."

"I'll tell you what, go downstairs, I'll change and join you in a minute. I'll make us some tea."

"Yes, of course. Thank you." He straightened his bow tie, smiled and turned to go down the stairs.

Five minutes later, I joined Eustace at the coffee counter. I'd stopped by Rosy's office and asked her to stay until Eustace left.

"I'm sorry to come in so late but it's been too loud and crazy here to work on anything," Rosy apologized.

"I get it," said the woman who passed out for four hours because it was "too loud and crazy here."

I patted her on the shoulder. "Thanks for coming back to work on the books."

I poured peppermint tea from a tea set my mother had bought me in England and handed him a cup. We settled into a table near the cafe counter.

"First, I'm so sorry about all of this. Showing up here. My nephew… ," his voice cracked.

"This must be so difficult for you," I said. "First your brother and now your nephew."

"Yes, it is."

"But you're going to keep the family home? And move in with Gabrielle?" I asked, reminding him of our previous conversation.

I knew something wasn't right earlier. Like he had something else to tell me but he just couldn't.

"That's who I'm here to talk to you about. I've been walking and trying to figure out what to do about Gabrielle."

"What do you mean 'do about Gabrielle'?"

"I think she murdered her husband." He smoothed his tweed jacket. "Should I tell the police?"

"Why do you suspect Gabrielle?" I asked.

"As much as I loved my nephew, he wasn't a nice

man. He did things to Gabrielle. He hurt her," he said, stumbling around instead of coming out and saying it.

"You mean he was abusive," I said even though we'd already covered this the first time he stopped by today.

He shifted nervously and took a sip of his tea before continuing. "Yes. I'm sure you've seen the video of my altercation with him beside the pool."

"Yes, Sage showed me. So you don't think my Aunt Mary killed him?"

"No, Mary has always been compliant with the historical society rules and easy to get along with." He set his tea cup on the saucer and pushed it away.

I didn't know what following historical society guidelines had to do with being a murder suspect.

I set my tea cup down and leaned across the table. I placed a comforting hand on his forearm. "Eustace, if you suspect Gabrielle. You need to tell the police everything. This isn't some infraction against the historical code, this is murder."

"Thank you," he said as he stood and put on his overcoat. "She asked me to drive her to the police station in the morning. I'll talk to them then." He buttoned his coat, straightened his bow tie, and smiled. "You've been most helpful."

After Eustace left, I told Rosy goodnight and climbed the stairs to my apartment. I pulled my phone out of my sweat pants pocket and texted Dexter.

Are you still awake?

He texted back:

You're supposed to be asleep.

I know. You're not going to believe who just stopped to visit me.

Who?

Eustace. He thinks Gabrielle murdered Horace. I told him to come talk to you. You're welcome.

Why does he think that?

I couldn't say. Trying to make sense of that is out of my depth

.

Okay. I get it. I apologize.

Talk tomorrow?

Yes. Goodnight.

I left the phone in the kitchen, climbed the stairs, and crawled into bed.

————

The next morning, Clare and Ashley arrived early for story hour again.

"I have a craft," Ashley said.

"Ashley, Clare, I have a lot on my plate right now. Would you two mind running story hour?"

"Do you mean for today or long term?" Clare asked.

I paused, replaying Edgar's advice in my head.

I tapped my finger on my forehead as Rory ran circles around the cafe. "How about for the next month? We'll revisit it then and see if you'd like to stay longer. I'll pay you, of course."

"No, you won't," Ashley said. "Story hour is free preschool for our kids."

"On one condition, actually two," Clare said. "You

help us pick out the story when we need help. You let us borrow an employee when needed."

"Done and done," I said.

Ashley hugged me. "Harper, we're really sorry, you know, with everything going on, it must be so difficult. You do so much for us, for everyone, every day."

Clare followed suit and said, "Yes, we're happy to help. Whatever you need."

As I wiped a tear from my cheek, I said, "Thanks. What's the craft for today?"

"Caterpillars out of egg cartons," Ashley said, opening her bag and showing me googly eyes and pre-cut egg cartons.

Theo and Dominic joined Rory running circles around the cafe. It was all great fun until Theo tripped and skinned his knee. Zoe saved the day with a wet paper towel for his knee and mini peanut butter muffins and hot chocolate.

With Theo and Dominic picking mini marshmallows out of their hot chocolate and eating muffins, the crisis was averted.

Ashley continued, "We don't need help picking the book today."

"*The Very Hungry Caterpillar*," we all three said in unison.

With Story Hour squared away, I filled Zoe in on what was going on and climbed the stairs to my apartment to work on my new novel.

As soon as I sat down at my desk, my phone buzzed.

Your Aunt Mary is here and so is the nerdy detective.

Before I could gather my thoughts and my things, Aunt Mary, it must have been her, punched in the code on my door.

"Harper, it's me," Aunt Mary said.

"And me," Dexter said.

I descended the stairs and went straight to Aunt Mary. "I'm so glad you're okay," she said as I hugged her.

"You're the one that was arrested for a crime you didn't commit," I said, glancing at Dexter, who said nothing.

"Let me make us some coffee and we can chat," she said.

"I need to get to work," Dexter said. "I was stopping to check on Harper."

"I think what Harper and I have to tell you will qualify as work or part of your investigation."

"I have to be at the station by nine-thirty. Gabrielle is coming in for questioning."

Aunt Mary put a hand on her hip. "I think we can make sure that happens."

Aunt Mary busied herself in the kitchen with the French Press while I filled Dexter in on everything on the murder board. Funny, yesterday afternoon, I'd played the exact same scenario with my mother and experienced a totally different outcome.

With Aunt Mary, I felt peaceful, safe, and strong. With my mom, I felt flawed, broken, and ashamed. And she took every opportunity to tell others what a weak and broken creature her daughter was. I filed those thoughts away to share with Edgar later in our session. I turned my attention back to the murder board.

"You can tell him about my past," Aunt Mary yelled from the kitchen.

"I think I'll let you share your backstory," I said.

"Full disclosure, your sister came into the police station yesterday and told us you killed your father," Dexter said.

"What?" Aunt Mary didn't say anything for about sixty seconds after that. "Harper, can you grab your laptop?"

I ran up to my bedroom and grabbed it. Once downstairs, I handed it to Aunt Mary. She typed in something and turned the screen towards us.

"My father is alive and well," she said. "This is for your investigation, not for public knowledge."

The website advertised: **Oliver Sterling, the enigmatic billionaire behind Sterling Innovations**

Dexter read the headline and added, "Your father is Oliver Sterling, the billionaire?"

"Yes," she said.

"Sterling Innovations: Elevating Luxury with Designer Clothing, Exquisite Jewelry, and Exclusive Home Decor for the Elite," Aunt Mary read the tagline of the website aloud.

"What if he's seen you on the news?" I asked.

"Don't be ridiculous," Aunt Mary snapped, which was uncharacteristic of her. "He's seventy-five. He's known where we were for years."

"Oh," I said. "Does mom know?"

"Of course not. Your mom is living in her little delusional world where I'm the villain and father is the victim. If you knew what he did to me, to her…" Her voice trailed off.

"Let's have that coffee," I said. "I'll ask Zoe to send up some scones."

We sat at the table. Aunt Mary shared that when her father had found them, a mere few months after they left, she threatened to go to the police and the press and tell them of the abuse. Whether they believed her or not, it would destroy his reputation.

Dexter folded his arms across his chest and leaned back in his chair. "The case of the kidnapping of the Sterling girls, it was all a ruse? It was in our textbooks at the academy."

"Yes," she said.

I grabbed my computer and typed in a search: kidnapping of the Sterling girls.

Thirty-four years ago, the Sterling girls, twenty-one and eighteen at the time, were kidnapped. Although Oliver Sterling paid the ransom, the girls were never returned. Presumed dead.

Photos of Aunt Mary wearing a designer pencil skirt and silk blouse and mom wearing pink plaid pants and pink cable knit sweater flashed across the screen.

"Why didn't you tell Mom?" I asked.

"You heard her yesterday," she said. "She would have run back home and done whatever father and mother said. I couldn't' let her…"

Curious to hear Aunt Mary's side, I pushed for more information. "She said you tried to kill your Father."

Aunt Mary straightened her back and retorted, "I confronted my father about molesting her and he had a heart attack. He hit his head on his desk when he fell. She ran in the room and found me over his body with blood soaking up the carpet from his head wound."

"You don't seem shocked," I said, studying Dexter.

"I'm a detective," he said. There was more to it, but I wasn't going to press the issue right now.

I wasn't the first in line when it came to family inflicting trauma. Apparently, I was a victim of the trickle down effect. "Aunt Mary, I think you need to talk to Edgar."

She sipped her coffee. "Yes, I think you're right. And so does your mother. She's blocked out whole chunks of her past and replaced them with her own version."

"You've carried this burden for so long," I said, standing and giving her a side hug. "You did the right thing rescuing mom and coming here, no matter what she says."

Zoe arrived with the scones and set them on the counter. After glancing at the murder board, she scurried back down the stairs.

I filled Dexter in on all the evidence I'd gathered and we removed suspects from the board including the landscaper, the caterer, the cameraman, and left some we still weren't sure about. So far the suspects with motive were as follows - Aunt Mary and Gabrielle. I left Aunt Mary on the board because according to Dexter, she wasn't in the clear.

Dexter checked his watch and excused himself.

Forty-five minutes later he texted me:

Gabrielle's been arrested for murder.

CHAPTER 11
PREMEDITATION AT THE COZY CORNER

I ADDED Gabrielle to the center of the board and placed Aunt Mary's photo on the side.

"I'm still on the board, huh?" she asked as she looked up from the book she was reading.

I patted her face in the photo, making sure it was secure on the board. "I'm only leaving you up there because Dexter says you're still a suspect. Of course I know you didn't do it."

Then I pointed to Gabrielle's photo. "I'm not sure about Gabrielle either."

She set her book down on the couch and stood and stretched. "You don't know her that well. She ignored you for years and shows up and embeds herself in your life? Some would call that premeditation."

"I've heard the same speech from Sage," I said. "I'm going upstairs to work on my novel."

She followed me to the bottom of the stairs. "The one you need your mom's help on?"

"Yes." I turned and faced her.

She gripped the handrail and paused. "I'm not a writer, so I don't know how your creative process works, but I suggest you shelve that one for now."

I studied her face for clues. "Why?"

"Your body is under a lot of stress as it is. Talking to your mom about Paris will bring to the surface a lot of emotions you may not be able to handle right now."

I had to admit that spending time with my mother was emotional to say the least. "You sound like Edgar."

She was right. I couldn't have a repeat of yesterday every day I worked on the novel. So it was back to the drawing board.

"I have one question about Mom. How could she not remember Grandpa Oliver?" I tried out the name for the first time.

"She suffered from dissociative amnesia after we left. I took her to doctors and psychiatrists. Although they were able to help her recover from her night terrors and fear, she still doesn't remember exactly who she is. Who we are. She created her own version of my father and her past."

"I want to write about that," I said.

"About our family?" she turned and went back to the kitchen to refill her coffee. "I don't think that's a good idea."

"No, not about our family. About some of these issues we've suffered or struggled with, agoraphobia, dissociative amnesia, and the effects of trauma. But you're right, not a good idea now." I didn't wait for her answer. Instead I ran up the stairs and grabbed my iPad. I started a new note and scribbled down ideas for a new cozy mystery.

I folded the iPad cover closed and turned to the computer to type a chapter of *The Evergreen Enigma.*

An hour and a half later, I stood and stretched. It was time for fresh coffee, and keeping Edgar's advice in mind, I would only stay in the bookstore long enough to say hello to The Classics, grab a coffee, and see if my employees needed anything.

The rest of the day ran smoothly in the bookstore. I used my hour and half out for another hike, this time with Sage, which felt good, like old times, the time before Gabrielle had inserted herself in my life. This time, I didn't suffer from anxiety swallowing me up. Sage had brought her camera along and we stopped here and there as she took photos of daffodils springing up. Our conversation felt warm and familiar.

"This beats hanging out with murderers," she said as she snapped a photo of me examining a daffodil.

"If you don't stop taking photos of me, there will be another murder," I said, rushing ahead.

I didn't want to talk about the case, my mother, my grandfather, or Gabrielle. Although I'd imagined myself being the sleuth who saved the day or confronted the killer as portrayed in my cozy mysteries, this wasn't a book. It was real life.

I'd been fooled by a murderer who had inserted herself in my life so she could murder her husband, fully expecting me to be the main character in my books and solve the crime. Only she didn't think I was intelligent enough to discover the real murderer. Her.

Knowing that Mom had been spreading the gospel of poor wretched broken Harper around the town, who knows what Gabrielle had heard and believed.

I threw my head back and looked up through the branches of the blue spruce which created a kaleido-scope with the sun shining through. I twirled around a few times like a child. It didn't matter what else was going on. Right now, I felt like the child I'd been meant to be. The child without a care in the world. The child whose parents hadn't chosen to abandon her for their career. The daughter whose father loved her. A scripture came to mind.

Dizzy from my twirling, I sat down on a rock.

"Do you pray?" I asked Sage.

"Sometimes," she replied while snapping more photos of daffodils.

I picked a daffodil and twirled it in my fingers. "I find myself praying more often now. I was just thinking of the scripture that says we've been adopted as God's children. I can't remember the exact verse."

She turned and took exactly ten photos of me. "The one in Ephesians 1 that says we were chosen before the foundation of the world to be adopted as His own."

I dropped my flower and sat up. "You speak Bible?"

Sage chuckled. "Have you met my mother?"

Sage's mother ran Graceful Gatherings Women's Ministry.

I said the name of the ministry and we both recited "is a place for women to connect, grow in their faith, and support one another in their spiritual journey" from memory.

She taught a weekly Bible Study for women. I'd

lived in the bubble of my building for so long, writing novels and running the bookstore, that I'd forgotten about other peoples' lives. Now that I was facing my past and my fears, I looked at the world through a different lens. A lens that was still blurred by my old beliefs. My muddled beliefs when it came to where I fit into the universe begged to be cleared up.

"Do you think when our parents don't want us, God still does?" I asked.

"Of course," she replied.

"I'd like either Edgar or God to be my father," I said while plucking some new blades of grass.

"You're different," Sage said.

"I am. I want to go to your mom's Bible study," I said.

Her watch buzzed. "Time's up in ten minutes, should we head back to the car?"

———

The next few days flew by. Things settled down and Evergreen Heights got back to normal. Aunt Mary, cleared of all charges, worked on the set of Sell It Or Stay. The show planned to resume filming the next week. Eustace agreed to take Horace's place on the show. As long as the contractor stuck to the historical guidelines in the final weeks, there would be less tension on the show. Aunt Mary and Eustace agreed to nix the hot tub by the conservatory. That alone would speed up the process.

Gabrielle, with Eustace's help, hired a high powered

attorney from the city. Once released, she showed up at book club.

"Hi Harper," she said, fiddling with her cuff.

"Hi, how are you?" I asked as I placed stacks of the newest book club book on each table.

"I'm doing well, I'm excited to discuss tonight's book." She smiled.

"Aren't you worried about the murder charge?"

She laughed. "Eustace says his lawyer will get me off. Don't you see, everything is working out. I get the house. Eustace plans on moving in with me. I can do whatever I want now."

Did she not know that it was Eustace who had turned her in?

The funeral for Horace was crowded. That's an understatement. The church overflowed out into the street with journalists, brought on by the show, Sell it or Stay. This may be the first time in reality G-rated TV that someone had been murdered during filming. The whole town attended, including me, not because Horace was well-loved but because the people of Evergreen Heights always attend funerals of the townspeople.

The repast couldn't be held in Horace's house, so instead, Eustace pulled some strings and rented the town hall. The people of Evergreen Heights, like most small towns, were famous for supplying baked goods, casseroles, and enough food for a small army. Today a small army showed up. I mingled with a few town's folks I knew well while Sage took photos for the newspaper.

After ten minutes, I ended up hiding in the corner behind a fake Ficus eating a brownie.

My mother reveled in the attention, as she stood in the center of a group of townspeople and shared about her travel plans with a spattering of "So sad to leave my broken daughter." Those weren't her exact words, but they should have been. She planned to fly out the following week. Her sister, my aunt, had been cleared of all charges, the show was finishing up… meaning there were no more opportunities to be on camera.

As my mother prattled on, I shifted my gaze to a few other townsfolk. Not one person seemed upset. Instead, this gathering resembled a party.

"Why are you hiding behind the tree?" Dexter asked, pushing the leaves aside and peeking at me.

"Observing. Why are you here? You didn't know Horace," I said, standing and dusting the brownie off the black funeral dress my mother had chosen for me.It hugged my hips and I felt as if it showed every lump and bump in my body. Another reason I was hiding.

"Observing," he said, mirroring my words.

I yanked at the skirt of the dress."You don't think Gabrielle murdered her husband do you?"

My watch buzzed. "I've got to get back to the bookstore."

"I'll walk you," he said.

Once outside, I didn't wait before I asked.

"Why don't you think Gabrielle murdered her husband?"

He pushed his glasses up his nose. "I didn't say that. You did."

"You're still investigating though. That's why you showed up at the funeral."

Dexter leaned over to tie his boot lace before straightening and adding, "Yes, I wouldn't be a great detective if I didn't complete a thorough investigation."

I slid my arm into the black trench coat my mother had provided. "Sage and my aunt say Gabrielle befriended me to give herself an alibi and a character witness."

Dexter grabbed the trench coat and helped me slide my other arm in. "You mean after years of abuse, she planned to murder her husband on the set of a reality TV show?"

"Sounds a little off," I said as I buttoned the coat and tied the belt.

"May I be blunt?" he asked.

He linked arms with me and we walked in the direction of the bookstore. "Your aunt said that Gabrielle was one of the, for lack of a better word, a mean girl when you were in high school."

"Yes," I said.

He slowed his pace as I struggled with the four inch heels my mother had insisted on my wearing. "Then she marries a Vanderhilt, endures years of abuse, befriends you all with the idea of a premeditated murder?"

I shook my head. We were standing outside of the bookstore now.

"Would you like to come in for a cup of coffee?"

"Yes," he said. "I would."

Once inside, I prepared our coffees. Everyone was at the funeral. I'd left one college student to man the store. She didn't feel competent enough to make espressos yet and the presence of the detective made her nervous. I excused her.

After our coffees were made, I said, "Let's go to the second floor. We can talk there." I handed him his cup. "Everyone will be back any minute," I explained.

Once seated on the leather couches, I said, "You were saying?"

Dexter leaned back on the couch and the leather creaked. "Whether Gabrielle killed her husband or not, she didn't befriend you because she'd been planning it."

I slid my feet out of my shoes, and tucked them under a pillow on the couch. "Why did she befriend me?" I asked, thinking he couldn't give me a logical answer.

"Let me offer a different perspective. Gabrielle for years is smothered by her husband's demands and abuse. When your aunt agrees to take on the remodeling project, and the cast and crew show up, Gabrielle has a bit more freedom. So she takes it. She comes and finds you, the girl who shared her lunch with her in middle school. Your aunt told me." He leaned back on the leather Chesterton sofa and sipped his coffee.

"Oh, that's a different perspective. What about premeditation?"

"Can you join me at the crime scene tomorrow and we'll walk through what happened? I promise you this crime wasn't premeditated."

"Yes," I said.

We set a time, finished our coffees while we chatted about books, and he left.

The next morning, as I was trying to decide what to

wear to a crime scene, my phone vibrated. Dexter. I picked it up.

"There's been a new development. There are two more bodies."

"Two more people were murdered?"

"I don't know."

"What do you mean you don't know?"

"It's two skeletons."

CHAPTER 12

DIGGING UP SECRETS AT THE COZY CORNER

IT WAS EARLY SUNDAY MORNING, the day before filming started again on the set of Sell It Or Stay. Joe, from Main Street Excavators, dug up two skeletons near the conservatory. Apparently, he hadn't gotten the memo to nix the hot tub and he and his crew were getting a head start before filming began again the following day.

I pulled out a pair of jeans from the back of the closet, something I didn't normally wear. Then I stuffed them back in. What did one wear to what was meant to be an inspection of a crime scene which had turned into another crime altogether? I'd planned to go to church this morning, but this visit to the crime scene would eat up all my time out today. Finally, I settled on the pair of sage trekker pants Gabrielle had purchased for me and a light pink sweater, and topped it off with a windbreaker.

I ran downstairs and bumped into Zoe. "What are you doing here on Sunday morning?"

"Everything has been so crazy here all week, I didn't get to give the cafe area a deep clean so I thought I'd do it while the bookstore was empty."

"Oh, thank you," I said.

"Where are you going in such a hurry?" she said, eyeing my wardrobe choice.

"I'm going to the set of Sell It or Stay," I said.

"Gabrielle's house?"

I zipped up my windbreaker. "The landscape crew dug up two skeletons."

"What?" She fiddled with a steam wand and dropped it in the sink. It landed with a loud clink. "That's crazy!"

"I know. Detective Dexter is there, I'm going to check it out with him."

"Want me to drive you?" She jingled her keys.

"No, I'll ride my bike."

A light fog covered the town, so I turned on my headlight. The sun resembled the Van Gogh rendition of *Starry Night* as it fought to burn through the fog. According to the mountain weather pattern, that meant the sun would win and we'd have a beautiful day in about two or three hours.

Ten minutes later, I arrived at Gabrielle's house. Blue and red lights blinked in the fog, announcing the crime scene. I parked my bike and Dexter joined me.

"Hello," he said.

"Hi." We walked through the wet grass, soggy beneath my feet.

"Glad you wore your rain boots. It's a mess back here." He led me to the ancient conservatory where a group of experts talked about the two skeletons which were covered by tarps. Sage was among them snapping photos of the mud around the bodies.

"I think I've got all we need," she said. Some of the crew moved forward and placed the skeletons on gurneys and wheeled them away. After they'd taken the bodies, she joined Dexter and me.

Sage kicked the leftover blue tarp."Can you believe it? Those bodies were buried under there all these years and no one knew it."

"Who were they?" I asked.

Sage replied,"I have no idea, but I can tell you this, one is a male and one a female. Also, I'd guesstimate they've been under the ground for at least a decade. That's not official, Dexter. I'm just talking."

"Of course," he said.

"What are you doing here Harper?" she asked.

I knocked into her arm with my shoulder."Nice to see you too. Dexter invited me here to reenact Horace's murder."

She overcompensated as she regained her balance and grabbed my arm."That's a messed up date."

"Dexter is not sure Gabrielle killed her husband."

"Well, I don't think she killed these two, whoever they are. She didn't know the Vanderhilts ten years ago, so no motive, right detective?"

"I guess we can't reenact the murder?" I said.

Dexter turned and looked around at the few officers left combing the scene."We can, let's go over to the garden shed and grab a shovel."

Five minutes later, Dexter walked us through Horace's murder. Sage filled in for Horace because she was almost as tall as him and so I could observe.

"You see, whoever murdered Horace didn't confront him from the front, she/he came behind him with a shovel and boom, hit him." He demonstrated. Sage stumbled forward.

"No defensive wounds," she added. "He's right. There was no altercation. Someone came up behind him and took him out."

"You said it wasn't premeditated," I added.

Dexter swung the shovel around for emphasis. "This isn't the sort of crime you plan for weeks or months. Someone was angry. Maybe they were talking and Horace turned around for a moment and the murderer grabbed the shovel and bam."

"Gabrielle still could have done it," Sage said.

"Harper, your turn," Dexter handed me the shovel. "You try."

Sage turned and I raised the shovel and brought it down in an arc. The shovel landed on her back.

"Ow, Harper, you weren't supposed to hit me." She stumbled forward.

"Sorry, I got caught up in the murder, I mean the moment."

"See," Dexter said, "That's what I mean and Horace had a good four inches on Sage. How tall is Gabrielle?"

"About my height?" I guessed.

"Two inches shorter than you," Sage said. "She wears heels all the time to appear taller."

There was a commotion near the squad cars.

"We've got to get back to work," Dexter said.

"Yeah, we do," Sage agreed.

Why did I suddenly feel jealous that my best friend was spending time with my... my what? My new friend? My I-think-I-like-this-guy-friend? The one I'd been leaving my safe building more in case we someday got married and had a family guy?

Dexter and Sage walked through the archway in the hedge and joined the commotion at the squad cars.

Dexter said firmly, "You can't go over there, Eustace, it's a crime scene." Dexter restrained him with one arm.

"What did they find?" Eustace asked as he broke from Dexter's grip.

"What do you mean?" Sage asked.

Eustace quickly switched gears and asked, "What was the crime?"

I wheeled my bike past the cars. While I inserted the key into the battery, Eustace continued his questions. Something didn't sit right with me. No matter how hard I thought about what it was, I couldn't put my finger on it.

I pedaled home, taking the long way so I could enjoy my last half an hour out. I'd asked Zoe to walk Rory before she left, so I didn't have to worry about taking him out until later. Uncharacteristically, the sun broke through the fog, and the day warmed up. I pulled over at the park to remove my jacket. I parked my bike and walked over to the gazebo. It was nice to enjoy the spring weather without the usual anxiety that normally plagued me. Could I get better? Edgar's regime seemed to be working. I'd been out and about for an hour and twenty minutes and I felt fine. Maybe there was hope for me.

The bushes behind the gazebo rustled.

"There you are," Aunt Mary said to me. "I've been looking all over for you."

"Why are you hiding in the bushes?"

"I dropped my phone," she laughed. "Here it is."

"Just getting ready to head back," I said. I couldn't have a lengthy conversation right now. My time was up. My watch buzzed in agreement.

"Right," she said. "Meet you back at the Cozy Corner. I have my car," she said, pointing across the street to her cream-colored Escalade.

"Okay!" I stood up, ran down the stairs, and grabbed my bike.

Five minutes later, I wheeled my bike inside and back to the storage room. Why was Aunt Mary acting so strange? Was there something she hadn't told me about my past? About my mom? I was spiraling and I knew it.

Zoe busied herself behind the cafe counter, cleaning the machinery.

Instead of asking her to make me a coffee, I said, "Tell my aunt to join me in my apartment."

"Will do. Oh, and I walked Rory while you were out. He's up there lounging on his pillow."

Aunt Mary ran in my apartment door, breathless.

"I heard about the bodies they dug up. There's something you need to know about Horace."

"What?"

She removed her jacket and draped it on the island. "The year before his father disappeared, they fought like cats and dogs. Eustace had to act as a mediator."

I picked her jacket up and hung both of ours on the coat rack. "But that's not what everyone in town says. They say he was heartbroken when his dad died and he changed."

She picked up the French Press and scooped coffee grounds in it. "That's not entirely true. He did change in some ways but he was always a contentious spoiled brat."

"What does that have to do with the skeletons?" I plopped a pod in the Keurig. Aunt Mary stopped scooping and set the press on the back of the counter.I didn't want to spend the time the French Press took. This conversation was more important than the strength of the brew.

As the machine hissed and spit out the dark rich brew, my aunt said,"I think the bodies are Horace's dad and the housekeeper he was in love with."

I handed her the first cup and the heavy cream. I peeled out the hot pod and added another one, grabbed a mug from the cabinet, and placed it on the base.

As my coffee streamed into my cup, Aunt Mary jumped up. "Where's your murder board? We now have three murders to solve and I think I know who committed the first two."

"Who?" I grabbed my freshly brewed coffee and joined her in the living room where she'd flipped the board over to the blank side.

"Text Sage and tell her to send some photos of the crime scene over. We need to start another board."

"We?" I asked.

She dropped the dry erase marker and grabbed my elbows. "There's something I didn't tell the police about Horace ten years ago. You were having all those issues. I'd suffered at the hands of my father and I had a feeling Horace experienced the same."

My coffee sloshed on the floor as she shook my

arms. I freed my arms from her grip, set my coffee down, and went to the kitchen to grab some paper towels. I rejoined her in the living room and sopped up the mess.

"What? What did you not tell the police?"

"The night before Horace's father disappeared, the night before Horace's twenty-first birthday…" She was rambling and repeating herself.

"Take a breath," I said. "Slow down." Our roles had reversed. I'd never had to calm Aunt Mary down. It was *her* job to calm me down.

She stopped, her shoulders rose and fell as she calmed herself. She grabbed her coffee and took a gulp.

"I saw Horace and his father arguing. Horace said he wasn't going to continue the family legacy and run the company. He was going to spend the family money on whatever he wanted."

"No offense, Aunt Mary, but that sounds like normal rich kid stuff. Not to mention, Horace did run the company for ten years and increased the profits."

"That's because he felt guilty. You didn't let me finish. Horace told his dad, 'If you don't get off my back, I'm going to kill you.'"

"Aunt Mary!" I answered. "You didn't tell the police this?"

In answer to my question, she grabbed Horace's photo from the other side of the board and placed it on the blank side.

"He did it. He murdered his father and the house-keeper and it's my fault he abused Gabrielle all those years."

She started to cry. "I thought he was being abused and finally standing up for himself."

"You looked at this story through the lens of your past," I suggested.

"What?" she said.

I patted her on the back as she wiped her eyes with the tissue she'd pulled out of her trouser pocket. "That's what Edgar would say. What else can you remember about the argument?"

"Eustace broke it up. Talked them both down. Then I left. That's all I know."

"Let's talk to Eustace then," I said.

I grabbed my phone and sent out two texts.

One to Sage:

Could you send me some crime scene photos?

Dexter:

My aunt has something to tell you about the bodies you found this morning.

Eustace preferred actual phone conversations to texts. Since Aunt Mary had a working relationship with him, I asked her to make the call.

She dialed and his voice mail picked up.

"Eustace, it's Mary. Listen, I need to talk to you about the bodies the landscapers dug up earlier this morning on your family estate. I think I know who they are and who killed them."

CHAPTER 13
MURDER THEORIES AT THE COZY CORNER

AFTER AUNT MARY left her blunt and to-the-point message on Eustace's voicemail, I printed the crime-scene photos Sage sent me.

Aunt Mary and I pinned photos to the new/old crime on the clean side of the board. After Sage sent the photos, she texted me:

The bodies are a male and a female.

Dead about ten years. That's all I know so far.

Why do you need to know?

I quickly filled her in with a series of paragraph long texts.

Our conversation ended with her texting:

Aunt Mary thinks Horace murdered his dad and housekeeper and buried them in the backyard?

Me:

Yes.

Sage:

Dang!

The rest of my Sunday filled up with conversations

with Aunt Mary, Sage and Zoe. We pinned Horace as the main suspect on the murder board, but were sure to include a few other men that I didn't know but Aunt Mary did.

I'd seen them around town and a few of them in the Cozy Corner, but not well enough to assign them a motive. The Classics knew everyone in town, so I made a mental note to join them on Monday morning and see what they remembered about the time of Horace's father's disappearance. No one said much about the housekeeper, Maria's family, so I wondered if anyone had contacted them. Or how much they were questioned ten years ago.

I texted Dexter and asked. He hadn't responded to the last two texts I'd sent. My old-self curled inwardly. *He's tired of you. He was only placating you by sharing some of the information with you. Now he has real work to do and he'd like you to leave him to it. He can't date a girl who has panic attacks and can't leave her building.*

Zoe texted me:

That geeky detective is here. He wants to come up.

The old-me thoughts disappeared in a puff of smoke.

Me:

Fine. Send him up.

Zoe:

Okay. He's on the way. I'm arming the security system and leaving. See you tomorrow boss.

Dexter knocked on the door.

"It's open," Aunt Mary called.

"I brought food," Dexter said. He walked in and sat

the takeout bags on the counter. "Sorry I didn't answer any of your texts, Harper."

"I'm sure you were busy," I said with a smile, my self-confidence suddenly slipping. I'd had this same conversation with my father on a weekly basis.

"You're not going to believe what the M.E. thinks…" he paused and turned his gaze to the new/old murder board. "And you know."

"Know what? Spit it out, Detective," Aunt Mary said as she peeked in the takeout bags. "I hope you got Harper her bacon avocado burger and sweet potato fries. Oh, you did. Go on now." As if he could have answered as she continued to grill him.

He ignored the comments about the food and said instead, "Those bodies were murdered. They are most probably Horace's father and the housekeeper."

"Well, if you'd returned Harper's texts, you'd have more information than that. We know that much."

Maybe my old-self was on to something if Aunt Mary was upset as well.

Dexter ignored her for a minute, which felt like an hour, while he examined the new murder board. The paper crinkled as I unloaded the takeout and the plates clinked as I took them out of the cabinets. Every little move, including my breathing, amplified as if it were plugged into a bluetooth speaker.

"How did you get all this evidence? How do you know all of this?" he asked.

"What we have, Detective, is history. Relationships. We've had real-life conversations with these people as well as witnessed others," Aunt Mary said as she jerked the buffet drawer open and grabbed some cloth napkins.

"Foods ready," I squeaked, feeling cracked by the tension in the room. I'd set the table and put the food on plates, adding my napkins Aunt Mary had thrown on the table, instead of the sandpaper-like take out ones. I was doing it again, trying to do all the right things so the tension would flee, just like I did with my parents. Snap out of it, Harper, my new almost-phobia-free self said and added, "Aunt Mary, maybe you could fill Dexter in over dinner."

After a brief stare down, they joined me at the table. "Thank you for dinner, Dexter."

Before Aunt Mary could jab him with another remark I said, "Aunt Mary, tell Dexter what you told me earlier, about the argument you witnessed."

I picked up my burger and shoved it in my mouth, taking a large bite, so Aunt Mary would have to take over the conversation. Or Dexter, who was looking at Mary with anticipation instead of picking up his burger. As Aunt Mary hesitated, Dexter adjusted his glasses exactly three times and I chewed my bite exactly ten times.

"All right," she said with a nervous chuckle. "I may as well get it over with."

She filled Dexter in on everything she'd told me earlier, including some details she hadn't told me, such as where the conversation had taken place - outside of the conservatory. Also, that Eustace had left the three of them standing there after repeated attempts to get Horace to calm down.

Aunt Mary finished with a sad sigh. "I should have

told the police what I'd witnessed ten years ago." She stuck out her arms toward Dexter. "Go ahead. Arrest me."

Dexter ignored her arms, which she held over her burger that was getting cold, for another five seconds.

When you struggle with agoraphobia, you become hypersensitive to how much time has passed. You tell yourself things like "I'll be home in five minutes. I only have to stay ten minutes," and other time-related encouraging words. While everyone else is comfortable living in time, it is, or should I say has been, a constraint to me, a harsh slave-master.

"Wait," Dexter said. "Did Eustace call the police about the argument?"

Aunt Mary dropped her arms. "I don't know. I went home. I didn't follow him. I had a child to get home to."

"That child was you?" Dexter asked, pointing a sweet potato fry at me.

"Yes, ten years ago I was struggling with my symptoms…." I took another bite of burger so I didn't have to finish the sentence.

"You aren't going to arrest me for failure to provide evidence?"

"I'll cross that bridge when I come to it. Right now, I'd rather have your help," Dexter said as he picked up his burger.

Aunt Mary opened her mouth to answer. Her phone buzzed, interrupting whatever she was going to say. She stood and walked into the living room, which was open to the dining room. My whole main floor was essentially one large room, aside from the laundry and half bath. We could hear her side of the conversation.

"Calm down Eustace…. I saw Horace threatening his dad…. Yes, I'm sorry. Let's talk in person…" Then she walked to the windows overlooking the street. "I see you…. Yes, I'll ask her."

"I'll go let him in," I volunteered.

"I can do it," Dexter said.

Aunt Mary stood and wiped her mouth with a napkin, leaving a smudge of her burnt orange lipstick on the mustard yellow floral design.

"No, for two reasons. One. Zoe armed the system and I need to type in the code. Two. He is freaked out enough. Imagine a detective greeting him after he found out his brother and housekeeper were murdered."

Aunt Mary dropped her napkin on the table and motioned for me to go let Eustace in.

As I exited the apartment and descended the two floors, turning on lights as I went, I couldn't get the picture of the stain on my napkin out of my head. These murders were a stain on the Vanderhilt name. Add to that the murder of his nephew, could Eustace recover and move on? On the main floor, I typed in the code, disarming the system and opened the main door.

"Oh Harper, this is terrible…" He shucked his rain coat off and shook it. The once sunny day had clouded over and rivets of water ran through the street as the rain pelted down with a vengeance.

I took his coat and hung it on the coat rack for customers. "Aunt Mary left you a message."

"I just listened to it, not twenty minutes ago. I wasn't able to take calls today."

I walked ahead of him, slowing when I realized he wasn't keeping up. "Why?"

His brown practical dress shoes squeaked on the hardwood floor, releasing the rain they'd soaked up on the sidewalk. "I may as well tell you since you've been so kind to Gabrielle. I took her upstate to see her mother who is in the state penitentiary."

I stopped at the landing of the first set of stairs and turned to him. "Oh, I didn't know." Meaning, I didn't know her mother was in prison.

"I paid the bail early instead of waiting for Monday morning. Your detective friend gave me permission to take her to see her mother before …"

He didn't finish the sentence.

"She goes to prison," I filled in for him.

"Yes," he said. "Her mother is being released in two months."

"By then their roles will be reversed," I said aloud, filling in what we were both thinking.

As we walked up the second set of stairs to the apartment, he added, "I had my phone turned off all day because Gabrielle's grandmother forbade her from seeing her mother. After she called me for the tenth time this morning informing me I was not permitted to take Gabrielle to visit her mother, I turned it off." He straightened his bow tie.

I opened the door to my apartment and motioned for him to go in. Aunt Mary and Dexter were munching on their sweet potato fries and had apparently made up in the seven minutes I was gone.

Eustace stepped past them and studied the board for

five seconds and crumpled to the floor in a brown tweed-suited heap.

CHAPTER 14

NEURODIVERSE AT THE COZY CORNER

AS EUSTACE REVIVED, Dexter moved him to the couch, and Aunt Mary offered him a glass of water.

"You've had quite a shock," she said.

"Yes, seeing them, knowing that…" He stopped.

Since Aunt Mary and I weren't therapists and Dexter would most likely want to question him, not comfort him, I texted Edgar:

911. Need help.

Edgar:

Are you okay?

Me:

Yes. It's Eustace. In my apartment. He just heard the news about the murder of his brother and housekeeper and passed out.

I wasn't okay. I was absorbing Eustace's emotions and feeling a load of grief on my chest mingled with a touch of panic. Eustace had told me in our last session that autistics are often labeled unemotional when sometimes they have the superpower of empathy. They feel, to an exponential degree, the emotions of those around them, which is why they often shut down and look blank.

While Aunt Mary tended to Eustace and apologized ten times while stroking his tweed-covered arm, I plopped into the reading chair in the corner and fought the emotions flooding me instead of letting them flow through me like Edgar had told me to. Dexter joined me, kneeling down on one knee.

"You all right?" he asked. "Today has been a lot."

"A little dizzy," I admitted. Why did I say that? Why didn't I just say "fine" like other people did, suck it up, smile, and be normal? Act neurotypical. Another word I learned from the research in the books Edgar recommended. A word I was the opposite of. Neurodiverse described me.

"Hey, I'm sorry I didn't return your texts earlier."

"That's okay," I lied.

"I was thinking about you all day."

I didn't know what to say, so I said nothing in response. Instead, I blurted out, "I kind of have an autistic superpower."

"Oh," he said. He pulled me gently from the chair. "I think it's bedtime for you."

"Mary, do you think you could help Harper change into some pajamas and get into bed?"

Aunt Mary looked in my direction. "Oh, Harper. This has been too much for you."

She patted Eustace on the shoulder reassuringly. "I'll be back."

Aunt Mary took over and led me the rest of the way

to the stairs. At the base of the stairs, I turned and said, "Why do you feel panicked, Eustace?"

Eustace's face rotated between shock and surprise.

"Ignore her, she's…" Aunt Mary didn't finish. "Let's get you to bed, shall we?"

I stumbled up the stairs, feeling more dizzy with each step. It had been exactly seven minutes since I'd started feeling dizzy, and I couldn't go home. I *was* home.

Aunt Mary wrestled my pajamas on as if I were a toddler instead of a full-grown woman. She said with a laugh, "Put your leg in here, Harper." My body wasn't cooperating because it was once again shutting down, and my brain was in overdrive.

When I was finally tucked in, Aunt Mary sat next to my bed. We could hear the muffled voices of Eustace and Dexter. She put my noise-reducing headphones on.

"Edgar is on his way." I wrestled the weighted blanket. "I need to let him in."

"Goodness, Harper. Lie still and rest. I know the code. If you're okay, I'll go downstairs and wait."

I shook my head in the affirmative, and she kissed my forehead. After she left, the room began to close in on me. I panicked and jerked the weighted blanket a little too vigorously, falling out of bed with a hard clunk. I hit my head on the edge of the chair Aunt Mary had dragged over to the side of the bed. The conversation below faded as if someone had turned down the volume. Someone dimmed the lights, and I sank into darkness.

I woke groggy and disoriented until I felt the comfort of my weighted blanket holding me in place so

I wouldn't disappear. The glow of Edgar's silver hair shone in the dim night light.

"Edgar," I mouthed. My mouth felt as if it were full of peanut butter.

He must have sensed my stirring because he answered, "How are you, Harper?" He handed me a water bottle and stood to help me into a seated position.

"What happened?"

"You passed out."

"Again," I rasped after taking a swig of water.

"Yes," he said as he flipped on another light.

"I panicked," I said, remembering my actions. "Edgar, Eustace felt panicked. I used my superpower."

"Of course he felt panicked. His whole world has imploded."

"Did you talk to him?"

"No, I didn't. He left when I arrived, and I came straight up here after Dexter filled me in."

"Dexter and Aunt Mary gone too?" I asked.

"Harper, it's two a.m.. You and I are the only ones in the building, besides Rory, who Dexter walked before he left." I looked toward the corner where Rory's dog bed was, and he instinctively raised his head.

"I'm afraid I'm getting worse," I said. Rory joined us and put his chin on the bed. I patted him.

Edgar patted my head as if I were a small child. "To the contrary, you're getting better."

"How can you say that?" I pulled my blanket up to my chin and rocked back and forth. Rory sank down on the floor at Edgar's feet, curled up, and went back to sleep.

"Because your aunt said earlier today you rode your

bike to the Vanderhilt mansion. Dexter said you didn't panic." Edgar sat down and leaned back in the reading chair and smiled.

"I didn't. I went to the park by myself afterward." I smiled at the memory.

"Let's talk about this later in our session, but I'll leave you with this—I've said it before, this building isn't your safety. I know you don't like to hear this, but it has kept you from the issues that are now coming inside your building."

"You mean murder?"

He chuckled. "No, Harper. Living."

"Are you leaving?" I asked.

"Yes, I'm seventy-eight years old, Harper. I can't sit up all night anymore. Sage is on her way."

"Oh, thank you. I didn't mean to sound ungrateful."

His phone buzzed. "It's Sage. I'll go let her in, and I'll see you for our session tomorrow."

He stood, grabbed his overcoat and hat, and added, "Get some rest."

Sage knew the code, so he didn't have to let her in, but it was evident he needed rest and wanted to get home.

When Sage joined me, she said, "Scoot over. I'm not sleeping on the couch downstairs and having you up here having an episode without me."

She removed her raincoat to reveal her flannel kitten pajamas, and I giggled.

She slapped me with a kitten-covered sleeve. "No judging."

She slipped into bed with me, and we were suddenly middle school girls on a sleepover, giggling and telling stories that began with "Remember when…" After half an hour of this, she said, "You know what we need?"

"Sleep?" I said.

"No, snacks and a good movie." She hopped out of bed and tromped down the stairs to raid my kitchen. I clicked on the TV and searched for one of our favorites, landing on *You've Got Mail*, which was really Aunt Mary's favorite, but Sage and I had watched it with her a hundred times, so it was comforting like my weighted blanket. It felt like home.

For the next two hours, we forgot about murders and skeletons and stuffed ourselves with more chocolate, Fritos, and hummus than should be legal, watched *You've Got Mail*, and recited every line.

By the time we settled in to sleep, it was five a.m.. While we were deep in slumber, the building alarm shrieked. Sage fell out of bed, and I sat up and pushed the weighted blanket off. Rory barked, running in circles around the room before taking off down the stairs.

"What the heck?" Sage said.

CHAPTER 15

IMMERSED IN MYSTERY AT THE COZY CORNER

RORY LED the way down the stairs, followed by Sage and me in our pajamas. The security company contacted the police and they were sending a squad car. I squashed the desire welling up in me to text Dexter. He didn't need to be dragged out of bed for this.

When Sage and I arrived on the main floor of the bookstore, all the lights were on. Rosy was standing at the code box, punching the buttons with fervor, sweat running down her face.

Sage took over and punched the code in.

"Sorry, ladies, I wanted to get an early start. I must have punched the wrong code in."

Rosy backed up and stood in the corner, head bowed in contrition.

I set down the dangerous Swiffer I was holding. Sage had already ditched her weapon, a small handgun she carried on her person for safety.

"What were you going to do with that, Harper, clean

someone?" Sage laughed and took her handgun from the table and stuffed it in a PJ pocket.

"It's okay, Rosy, this is nothing compared to the last few days. Why did you come in early?" I asked.

She nervously ran her fingers through her silver-streaked raven hair. "I'm leaving early today, remember? I'm going to visit my son."

I pulled the tie on my robe tighter. "Oh, yes, I forgot."

Rosy smiled an apologetic smile and scurried back to the office, leaving Sage and I to deal with the police.

"And you hired her because…" Sage left the rest of the sentence hanging.

I ran my fingers through my curls before digging a hair tie out of my robe pocket. "She does a great job," I replied as I leaned over to put my hair in a messy bun.

Sage reached over and straightened my crooked messy bun. "She's kinda creepy and way too nervous. You're letting her leave early to visit her son?"

"Her son is in prison," I whispered.

"Why does that not make me feel any better?"

"She spent twenty years raising her children and now she's ready to join the workforce."

The rest of the conversation would have to wait. Blue lights flashed in front of the store. An officer opened the door.

After a minute of conversation, he checked the cash drawer which was empty (our practice). While he investigated, his word, not mine, I thought about the fact that society makes it difficult for stay-at-home moms to re-enter the workforce.

As if they aren't qualified to work any more because

raising kids turned their brains to mush. The opposite is true, especially for someone like Aunt Mary who had to homeschool me, arrange the environment to make sure I felt safe, manage the shopping, cooking and everything else.

That's why I gave Rosy the job. She'd raised four children. It wasn't her fault one of them was in prison. Rosy wasn't creepy, she was embarrassed and self-conscious. She felt as if it were her fault that her son was in prison. That's what she told Edgar, who then told me. I think the shame and guilt made her work harder than she should.

The officer, satisfied it was a mistake, left.

Sage and I climbed the two sets of stairs to my apartment like sloths, dragging our legs up each step.

"I need coffee, can you make the strong stuff?"

"Sure," I pulled the French press off the back of the counter and got busy while Sage went upstairs to take a shower. Once Sage left, I planned to write another chapter of the cozy mystery *The Evergreen Enigma*. It was time for Emma Hawthorne to discover a body.

Strange how no matter what was going on in my life, I could sit down and write for hours. The deep work only took a few minutes for me to sink into as the world faded away. This was the only occasion in which I had a difficult grasp of how much time was passing. I'd look up and realize three hours had passed when it felt like minutes.

One morning, Aunt Mary had popped in for a visit during the middle of a writing session. I'd served her some coffee and a cinnamon roll, telling her I needed to finish a scene and I'd be right back.

"I have to leave in an hour, so you have plenty of time," she had said, grabbing an art magazine mom had sent me and settling into the sectional.

When I'd finished the scene, stood up and stretched, and gone back downstairs, Aunt Mary had been slipping her coat on.

She had smiled. "It's been an hour and a half, Harper."

"Oh, sorry, I get lost in my writing," I'd said.

"That's a good thing. Maybe use a timer when you have company."

After a promise for her to join me for dinner, she'd left and I've used a timer ever since. Aunt Mary and Rosy weren't too different. Rosy visited her son in prison. Vivacious, outgoing, Aunt Mary visited me in the prison of my own making.

I wonder if I tried writing somewhere else if I'd have the same result. Maybe I could write at Bea's Bakery across the street to try it out. Just not today.

Sage, freshly showered and dressed, grabbed a Yeti out of my cabinet. "Borrowing this!" she yelled. "Pour me some of the good stuff."

The Yeti was one of the many gifts well-meaning friends had bought me so I would get outdoors more. Turns out, I might actually use it now.

"Bring it back," I ordered. "Sage," I added as I filled the insulated cup. "Thanks for coming over in the middle of the night and staying with me."

She smiled. "Like old times, wouldn't have missed it. What are you doing for your time out today?"

"I don't know, take a nap on a park bench?" I chuckled.

"Well, I'm going to work on the rest of the crime scene," Sage said as she put her coat on. "I'm going to write up some notes, enlarge some photos…"

"What are you thinking?" I said.

"How about you join me in my lab later and use that murder mystery mind?"

I handed her the Yeti she had set on the counter. "You mean find some more clues?"

"Yes."

"I'm in."

"Should I pick you up?"

"I think I can ride my bike five blocks."

She checked the lid on the Yeti, swung her overnight bag over her shoulder, and said, "See ya later, this is going to be so fun!"

I had an appointment with Edgar at noon, after The Classics broke up their daily meeting. It worked out perfectly for Edgar, he didn't have to make another trip to meet me. Plus we could eat lunch together.

"How about three?" I asked as she opened the door.

"Perfect, see you then."

I poured myself a mug of coffee and headed up to my office. I set a timer and worked on my novel for two hours. When the timer buzzed, I got dressed in a blue dress littered with daisies and added yellow lace up boots. I threw my unruly hair up in a bun again and went down to check on Ashley and Clare. They had agreed to run the story hour, but I didn't feel right if I didn't at least check on them and see if they needed anything, including holding a baby or entertaining a toddler, who I had the most interesting conversations with.

Ashley sighed with relief when she saw me. "Harper, I forgot the snack for the kiddos and Peregrine is fussy."

"What do you need me to do?"

"Could you hold Peregrine while I run across the street and see what the bakery has?" She shoved Peregrine in my arms, who looked at me with wide eyes and then let out a blood curdling wail. I turned to tell Ashley we could call the bakery, but she was gone.

I put Peregrine on my shoulder so he couldn't see my face and walked around the tables. His wail quieted to a body-quivering sob.

Dominic followed me giving me advice. "He likes if you bob up and down," he demonstrated.

Taking his advice, I bobbed and walked. Within a minute, Peregrine was asleep. I knew that to be true, because I checked in a mirror when I walked by. I didn't dare stop my bobbing and walking dance, for fear he would wake up, so I kept going.

I bounced and bobbed to the cafe counter. "Zoe, get this young man a hot chocolate. He deserves it for being so helpful."

"Coming right up," she said.

Instead of sitting down and drinking hot chocolate and basically fading into the background like kids did in Hallmark movies, Dominic and Theo followed me around like ducks, quacking about their latest games and toys.

"Yeah, we have this game we play," Theo said.

"I'm the ghost," Dominic added.

"I'm the ghost buster."

"Is this a video game or real life game?" I asked while continuing to move.

"Both," Dominic said. "Mom only let me download it on the iPad because you have to move to get the ghosts."

"You have to move?"

"Yeah, like this," Theo said, pretending to hold an iPad and running around the tables. "Then you see a ghost, you push buttons and zap him."

Dominic zipped around a table."But we play in real life too, because Mom says we can't have too much screen time."

"Harper, you gotta hear this. The game will melt our brains like the ghosts melt," Theo added, pretending to zap Dominic.

Ashley bustled through the front door, carrying a box of what I assumed were Bea's kid-friendly mini protein muffins. Clare had been busy setting up the craft upstairs while Audrey slept in a baby sling.

"I hope they weren't too much," she said. "Oh, he's asleep." She set down the box and whipped out her phone and took exactly ten photos of me and baby Peregrine. Then turned and took ten of Theo and Dominic who had continued the conversation without me, while holding hands.

"Do you want me to take him?"

"No, he's fine. I'll just keep walking around. You go do what you need to do."

She called Dominic and Theo to come drink their hot chocolate while she picked out a book. The boys sat at the counter, filling in Zoe on their ghostbusters game and it hit me how much they resembled The Classics in younger form. I guess conversation is the soul food we need at every age and stage.

I held baby Peregrine for an hour more as he snoozed peacefully on my shoulder and two story hours went off without a hitch. By that I mean the craft and story were a hit and the kids were loud and crazy at certain points as usual. No one showed up for the third hour which gave us all a moment to breathe. I consulted Ashley and Clare and we decided to remove the third story hour from the schedule since the weather was warming up. More moms would be doing outdoor activities.

Something had shifted in me while I held the baby. Instead of thinking about what I was afraid of, I thought about Clare and Ashley.It started as the smallest spark of empathy when I saw Rose fumble and trigger the alarm. She was flustered and ashamed for needing time off to visit her son in prison. That spark grew as I thought about the other moms, each carrying their own heavy burdens and juggling responsibilities that never seemed to ease. Seeing and feeling how exhausted the moms were who pushed through anyway for their kids, whether it was iPad limits, procuring mini protein muffins, dragging themselves out of bed to come to story hour— these women were heroes of their own story. It was about time for me to be a hero of mine.

I'd shut off feeling for so long because I couldn't regulate or recognize my emotions. Now it felt as if a fire hose had been turned on and I was feeling all the feelings. Edgar was right. Life was coming into my building and finding me and I was determined to participate and enjoy it.

CHAPTER 16
A FRESH PERSPECTIVE AT THE COZY CORNER

AFTER CLARE and Ashley packed up and left, I went back upstairs to my apartment. Before I sat down to write, I made a double shot so I didn't fall asleep face first on my keyboard.

Double shot in hand, I climbed the stairs to my office and stood in front of the window overlooking the street. Was the sun brighter today?

Usually after episodes like last night's, I suffered from a mild headache for a few days and grogginess. Today it was quite the opposite. Sure, I felt tired. I also felt light, airy, and alive.

Instead of working on my latest cozy mystery, I pulled out my iPad and sketched out a new book series with a mom as the protagonist. Still a cozy mystery, but instead of a single career woman, a mother. I'd written:

Protagonist Name: Lila Thompson

Character Synopsis: Lila Thompson is a dedicated wife and mother of two energetic young kids, balancing the demands of family life with her passion for community service. With a warm heart and a keen eye for detail, Lila volunteers at various local organizations, from the school PTA to the neighborhood watch. Her involvement in these activities puts her in the midst of the town's happenings, often placing her at the scene of mysterious deaths. With a knack for solving puzzles and a tenacious spirit, Lila becomes an amateur sleuth, using her insider knowledge and connections within the community to uncover the truth behind each murder. Her sharp intuition and empathetic nature make her a beloved figure in her small town, as she juggles family duties and crime-solving adventures with grace and determination.

Title: *Murder in the Neighborhood*

Summation: In the quaint town of Maplewood, Lila Thompson's life revolves around her family and community service. When a prominent local figure is found dead at the community center, Lila's curiosity and keen observation skills draw her into the investigation. As she juggles playdates, PTA meetings, and solving a murder, Lila uncovers secrets that threaten to unravel the peaceful facade of her beloved town. With the help of her supportive husband and a close-knit group of friends, Lila must navigate through a web of lies and deceit to catch the killer before they strike again.

When my phone buzzed at eleven forty-five, it felt as if only a few minutes had passed. I smiled and stood. This book is going to be so fun to write. As I brushed my teeth and redid my bun, I cataloged townspeople and traits I planned to use.

Edgar waited for me at the same table The Classics sat at every day.

"I ordered us some lunch from The Sandwich Shop," he said. His eyes were as wide as the dessert plates we served cinnamon rolls on. "You look chipper."

"I am. I started writing a new book today."

"Yes, but you write books all the time. This is something different."

I sipped the water bottle I'd grabbed from the fridge. "I feel different. You're right. Life is coming to the bookstore. I think it was all along but I was too closed off to see it."

"Well, then." He reached over and patted me on my shoulder as if I were a small child. I felt like a small child. Like Dominic and Theo sharing with me with such excitement and wonder.

After our food delivery arrived, while we ate, Edgar explained to me why the episodes were becoming more frequent. The more I participate in activities outside of my comfort zone, the more I have to be prepared.

My shoulders slumped. "You mean I'll always have episodes?"

Edgar patted me on the hand. "I didn't say that. I don't know. What we need to work on now is recognizing the precursor to the episode and making sure you have the tools to lessen the impact or stop it altogether."

I perked up at the suggestion that I could have some control. "Like what?"

Edgar leaned back in his chair, stretching his legs

underneath the table and crossing his arms. "I don't know yet. For now, you're going to be the detective in your own life. For example, what set you off last night?"

"We - Aunt Mary, Dexter, and I were talking. There was a lot of tension. I set the table nicely so they would calm down."

Edgar raised his hand to stop me. "You set the table nicely so they would calm down," he said repeating my words. "Harper, people don't calm down because you set the table nicely. Did you do this when you were younger?"

"Yes, when I was twelve and I spent the summer with my parents, I tried so hard to be who they wanted me to be. Learn the formal table settings," a torrent of tears burst like a block of ice freed from a waterfall. I put my face in my hands and sobbed. "And I was never good enough to pay attention to."

"Harper, your parents decided to pursue their careers and lifestyle. That was their choice. It doesn't mean you aren't good enough. It means they chose not to notice you."

I grabbed my napkin and swiped at the tears, willing them and the feelings to disappear.

The knot in my stomach tightened and I fought the urge to run upstairs and climb under my weighted blanket and stay there *forever*.

"If you're okay, let's finish. What happened next?"

"Well, we… oh…. I forgot one thing. Dexter ignored all my texts that day."

He drummed the table with his fingers. "I see. The tip of the iceberg. Continue."

I sipped my water."We discussed the murder board and then Eustace showed up."

"You said Eustace panicked," Edgar said, leaning forward.

I sat up straighter, thinking of how I felt the night before."Yes, I felt all these feelings emanating from him. Grief. Shame. But the one that surprised me the most - panic."

"Instead of honing in on his feelings, one of the coping mechanisms I'm going to teach you is the bubble." Edgar interlaced his fingers and pushed his arms in front of himself, as if he were prepping to play a sport.

For the next fifteen minutes, Edgar talked me through imagining there was a bubble enveloping me when the people around me were experiencing strong emotions or there was too much tension. He finished our session by assigning me some journaling exercises.

He hugged me and left. "You're making great progress."

I spent the next hour greeting and helping customers, which was one of the reasons I had taken over the bookstore, to talk about books.

Aunt Mary stopped and checked on me. The Sell It Or Stay show had decided to start filming episode two since number one was still on hold until the police gave the all clear. Dexter texted me and asked if he could stop by later in the evening.

At two forty-five, I wheeled my bike outside, released my hair from the bun, shoved my helmet over unruly curls, and rode to Sage's studio.

"You're not going to believe this," she said, pointing to three photographs hanging on a string.

"Hello to you too," I replied.

She turned and gave me a tight squeeze. "I've been waiting all day to show you this."

Grabbing a ruler, she pointed to a portion of each photo. "Each one of these have the exact same indentation in the skull, as if they were all hit with the same blunt object."

"You mean the same shovel?" I asked, moving in closer to study each indentation.

Sage folded her arms across her chest with satisfaction. "That's exactly what I mean."

I pulled Horace's dented head photo off the string. "So Gabrielle used the same shovel that Horace killed his father with."

"I don't think Gabrielle killed Horace. Remember the little demonstration Detective Poindexter had us participate in. She's too short and too, I don't know. You're the word person." She pointed the ruler at me.

I pretended as if I were typing on my computer. "Dainty. Wispy. I could go on for hours."

"Wait, you hiked with her that day. Did she have dirt under her fingernails or any broken nails?" Sage swung the ruler around and pointed at my hands.

"No, she looked perfect as usual. Not only that, she'd bought us hiking gear at Tom's Sporting Goods that day, brought them to my place, and we got ready together. I didn't see any mud or dirt on any of her clothes or body."

She smacked herself on the head with the ruler. "I'm right. It wasn't her."

"Now we're back to square one. Horace killed his dad and housekeeper Maria. He couldn't kill himself in the exact same manner," I said.

Sage set the ruler down and pulled the two indented skull photos off the string and studied them. "Maybe someone else murdered all three of them."

I plopped down in a chair. "Can you come over tonight so we can talk about this with Dexter? He texted me and said he wanted to come over."

"I don't think he wants to come and discuss the murder board," she giggled. "I think he wants to be alone with you."

A hot flush crept up my neck and continued to my forehead. "Even if he wants to be alone with me, we need to solve this murder. What if it is a serial killer?"

"A serial killer who kills in the exact same spot, with the same weapon, a decade apart." She put down the ruler and made her way to her coffee station.

"Coffee?" She plunked a pod in her Nespresso machine, knowing my answer to coffee is always "Yes."

"You're right. I feel like we are missing something. What are we missing? Gabrielle inherits the estate, but after getting to know her, I don't know that she's into all this status stuff." I fiddled with the fabric of my daisy dress.

"Have you seen her wardrobe?" Sage said as the machine hissed, pushing out the strong brew.

"I mean, she likes the money and clothes, but she's genuine. I can't explain it." I stood and took the coffee from her.

After taking a sip I added, "Eustace is moving in

with her, but doesn't he have his own house and money? I think he's just being kind."

"Oh," Sage said as she brewed another pod. "I guess so. His life is pretty great and busy with his law practice and the historical society. Maybe he feels sorry for her."

"Yes, he was around when Gabrielle grew up and he remembers the hardship her mother put her through. He took her to see her mom the other day."

I sipped my coffee, studying the skulls. "That's what we need to do." I jumped up sloshing my coffee on the cement studio floor. "We need to talk to people who were connected to the family ten years ago. Who stands to gain today as much as ten years ago?"

"You're right," she said. "We were too involved in our own lives to pay attention ten years ago. I was away at college and you were…" She let the words trail off instead of saying incapacitated. "So we need to interview people who were paying attention."

"I have an hour left. Should we get started?"

"Yes, my part-time boss at The Evergreen Times contacted me today to do a story on the old murder. So, this is work."

"And investigating at the same time. Let's go catch a killer," I said as I stood and swished my unruly curls before shoving my bike helmet over them.

CHAPTER 17

JENNY MURDER AT THE COZY CORNER

MY GRAND IDEA of catching a killer evaporated into a puff of disappointment.

Most of the people we stopped to talk to didn't remember, a few didn't live here then, and many people didn't care. Forty-five minutes later, we had nothing.

I sat down on a park bench. "We're doing this the wrong way," I said.

Sage frowned and her brows crinkled into what looked like two very hungry caterpillars."What do you mean?"

I took in a deep breath and blew it out before continuing."Well, you're used to taking an assignment and photographing on-site. And that's great. But what we need to do is research first, interview later."

"Where do we start?"

"The library." I glanced across the street. "We look at old newspaper articles and blogs. Oh… what about Crimecaster, the podcast about murder cases?"

Sage pulled out her phone and tapped on the

podcast app. "Jenny Murder host of Crimecaster. Found it."

"If that is really her last name I'm jealous. Why didn't I get a cool last name? Like the author Joanna Penn."

She grinned and joined in on the name game. "Or the pastor we listen to, Russell Moore, Moore to the Point."

"I have bad news," she added. "We just wasted five minutes of your time talking about names."

I glanced at the Evergreen Public Library. "The library has always been one of my safe places so I think I can extend it for a few…'

Sage shoved my helmet back on my head and buckled it loosely. "Not today. Not after last night. You shouldn't push it just because you feel good right now."

"You sound like Edgar," I said with a smile, already standing and pushing my curls down with my helmet. "I'll go back home and check out the podcast, and find all I can online. You go to the library and look up old articles."

I swung my leg over my bike and Sage waved and crossed the street.

"Come over later," I yelled.

"I'm not coming to your date," she yelled back. With her hand on the door to the library, she turned. "Reconvene tomorrow. Text me."

Back in my apartment, I grabbed my headphones and scrolled through the episodes of Crimecaster and found an episode pertaining to the "Clive Vanderhilt and Maria the help murder" which the police had deemed a disappearance.

Jenny reported in an upbeat voice, *"And I believe the*

police may have missed some evidence. I think Clive, along with his lovely housekeeper/lover was murdered. That's all Crimecasters, watch out for new episodes on the crime when I dig into the evidence. Signing off for now, Jenny Murder."

As I scrolled, I found zero more episodes. What happened? She had loads of episodes on other crimes, some she'd helped solve, skyrocketing her listenership to the top crime podcast in the United States. She'd gotten a book deal and written not one, but three books about three of the most difficult cases she'd podcasted about and helped solve.

My phone buzzed. I picked it up. Zoe's face appeared and I clicked join. This was strange. Zoe usually called or texted me. Not Facetime'd me.

"You have to come down here right now. You're never going to believe who is here." She swung her body around to show me *who*. She stopped and took exactly five photos of herself and Jenny Murder, who was perusing a stack of my novels.

Zoe jumped up and down, her spiral curls bouncing with joy. "I can't believe she's here! I've been listening to her podcast since I was sixteen."

"I'll be right down!" I clicked the hangup icon. What were the chances of Jenny Murder showing up in our small town? Skeletons were the chances. Those were proof that she'd been right all along.

I slid up beside Jenny. I didn't want her to think I was some sort of deranged fan, so instead of saying "Hello, I'm Harper," I cleared my throat.

She looked up from the novel she'd been reading and said, "Oh, my gosh Harper Deveraux. You're here." She swung her head around in an arc, taking in the bookstore. "Are you hosting a book signing or something?"

I smiled while I tried to figure out what to do with my hands. I put them in my pockets and pulled them out, before interlacing them behind my back. "No. I own The Cozy Corner Bookstore."

"Yes, I know," she smiled, her chocolate curls bobbing. "I'm your biggest fan. I mean you have a mind for murder like no other current writer."

"Except for you," I added.

"No, I just interview people and put together clues like they are a puzzle. No book signing?" She sounded disappointed as she gave my dress the once over. She looked down at her ripped jeans and black Doc Martens.

"She always dresses like that," Zoe shouted from behind the cafe bar. "And she's here literally all the time."

Thank you Zoe for not telling her I'm agoraphobic, but with Zoe's track record that information wouldn't be far behind.

"I can sign your books for you." Then I said what Zoe had been waiting to hear. "How about a few photos for our social media, the two sleuths?"

"Yes, please," she said.

Before I had time to beckon Zoe over she was in front of me, phone in hand, snapping photos of me signing the books, Jenny and I with arms around each other like we'd known each other for ten years instead of ten minutes.

"What are you doing here?" I asked through my

pasted-on smile for the fiftieth photo. "I think that's enough, Zoe. Thank you."

"Jenny Murder, here in The Cozy Corner Bookstore, right here in–"

I cut Zoe off with, "How about you make us some drinks?" Then I turned to Jenny. "Want to join me upstairs for a chat?"

Jenny asked for a lavender latte and I asked for a cold brew over ice.

"To your apartment or the second floor?" Zoe asked, grinning like the joker.

"You live here? I assumed you lived in one of the swanky houses like the Vanderhilts." Jenny did another scan of the bookstore. Did she think I slept on a bookshelf?

After another I-don't-know-what-to-do-with-my-hands episode, I leaned on the table housing my latest novel.

"Nope, I live on the top two floors of this building and Zoe is right, I'm here all the time. I write upstairs. I come down and help with the day-to-day."

"I get it. My studio is in my house. Sometimes I feel as if I never leave my house and have a social life. Do you ever feel like that?"

"She feels like that all the time," Zoe yelled over the noise of the coffee bean grinder.

"Yes, bring them to the apartment, please." The sooner we got upstairs, the quicker we could sit down and chat about the one thing that was on both of our minds - *murder*.

Just when I thought we were in Zoe-free zone, Jenny

turned and said, "Hey could you come upstairs and take some more photos in Harper's apartment?"

I glanced at Zoe who was obviously posting some photos that she'd just taken instead of making our drinks, evidenced by the phone in her hand.

"Sure, yes!" she squealed.

"That's okay right?" Jenny hesitated. "I mean, do you let your employees in your apartment?"

I laughed, Jenny obviously had a distorted view of me. "Zoe doesn't just work here, she's been one of my good friends for years."

As we climbed the stairs, I hoped I'd left my apartment clean and my bed made. I had a strange habit of not being able to leave the apartment unless the kitchen was spotless. Sometimes, after an episode, all of my cleanliness went to pot and I couldn't remember to eat food or drink water, much less wipe the counters.

"This is amazing!" Jenny said as I ushered her through the front door. "It looks like something from a Home.Health.Family. Network renovation show. Oh, yeah, Your aunt has a new show coming out, Sell It Or Stay!"

"Thanks, Jenny!" I replied, smiling. "I wanted it to be a space where I could relax and also entertain friends."

"The kitchen is fantastic," Jenny said, walking over to the hunter green cabinets. "And that stove! A pumpkin orange stove? It's like a perfect blend of retro and modern."

I laughed. "Yeah, it's a remake of a classic design. I thought it would add a bit of character."

"It definitely does," Jenny agreed, moving towards the long island with its crisp white countertop.

Jenny then glanced at the living room. "And this cream sectional looks so comfy! The orange and green accents really tie everything together. It's so inviting."

"I'm glad you like it."

"Like it? I love it!" Jenny said, sinking into the sectional. "I can see myself spending a lot of time here. You've done a wonderful job, Harper."

Jenny moved through the apartment, making herself at home and admiring the art on the walls. "Oh yeah, your mom is some globetrotting art expert. Your dad too. You got the gene jackpot. I love this…"

By the time Jenny had taken me on a tour of *my apartment,* Zoe arrived with not only the drinks but Sage and her camera in tow.

"I thought we'd get some proper photos," Zoe explained as she set the drinks down on the kitchen counter.

"I'm over at the library researching old newspapers in the dark, moldy basement, and you're here hobnobbing with Jenny Murder. I thought you were listening to an episode of Crimecaster, not interviewing the host."

Jenny picked up her coffee and took a long sip, staring at Sage wide-eyed.

Sage straightened her camera strap and stuck out her hand. "Sage Foster, forensic photographer. I'm working on the Vanderhilt case."

Jenny choked and snorted coffee out of her nose. Zoe handed her a napkin and she blotted her retro blazer. "Are all of your friends involved with murder?"

"Not me," Zoe said. "I've never murdered anyone. I just make the coffee," she giggled.

"We haven't murdered anyone," I said reassuring Jenny who was currently trapped in my apartment with what she thought were crazy people obsessed with murder.

Oh, and one of us was an agoraphobic, not sure how that fit in except for the fact that in murder cases, the police always dug up some trauma from the perpetrator's past. Trauma? Check.

Jenny laughed as she dabbed the last bit of coffee from her tee shirt. "You guys are the coolest people ever! I'm so glad I came. I mean, I thought, small town, it's going to be so boring. And this…." she waved her arms around. "This is what I've been looking for."

"Looking for?" I asked.

"Yes, I've been looking for a new town to relocate to. I've lived in New York City my entire life, but my mom died last year. It's time to cut the ties and find somewhere new and less expensive. Are small towns less expensive?" she asked while eying the *art* and *gifts* my parents had brought me from around the globe.

Zoe assured her Evergreen Heights was less expensive than New York City with a chuckle.

———

Exactly an hour later, Sage had taken three hundred photos. Sage had loaned Jenny a graphic tee she'd left here, so she could change out of the coffee stained one she'd been wearing since she snorted the coffee out of her nose. Under Zoe's direction, we posed *naturally* in my living room, kitchen, and office.

I leaned forward, bending at the waist like a rag doll. I'd had enough photo shooting to last me a lifetime. "Really, what are you going to do with all these photos, Zoe?"

"Social media baby." Zoe snapped her fingers and twirled around.

She'd left the cafe in the hands of a few college students and with the evening crowd of die-hard coffee drinkers quickly approaching, I suggested she go back downstairs.

Zoe hesitated. "One last thing, can we film a reel with all three of you?"

"What would we say?" I asked.

"Just say you're working on the Vanderhilt case together," Zoe suggested as she reached over and straightened my collar.

"Are we?" I looked back and forth between Sage and Jenny.

"Yes!" they both said.

"I'm not good on camera," I said.

Jenny flipped a chocolate curl off her forehead. "How about Sage and I do the talking?"

Turns out because reels are only a minute, Zoe decided we should do three of them. Not that I didn't have to be on social media for my author career, but Zoe handled all of that for me and my aunt.

We'd just finished the last reel when Dexter walked in the door we'd forgotten to close.

"Oh, am I interrupting something?"

Zoe said, "I've got some great reels, I'm going now."

Sage moved forward while I stood frozen. I couldn't believe it. Between keeping count of the photos and the time it took to take them, I'd forgotten my appointment, date, whatever, with Dexter.

I shoved my hands in my pockets. "Detective Dexter, this is Jenny Murder, host of the Crimecaster podcast."

"Detective?" Jenny said with a grin.

"Detective Dexter is working the Vanderhilt murder case, both of them," Sage said.

"I just fell more in love with this town," she said, giving him an appreciative once-over.

No. Jenny. He's mine. Where did that come from?

"Claws in Jenny, he's here for a date with Harper," Sage said, handing Jenny her blazer. "Let's go."

Jenny shoved her arms in her blazer. "Just when things were warming up. Oh, I wanted to tell you something, I guess the detective needs to hear this too."

We stood around the kitchen island littered with our coffee cups. I pushed aside the urge to clean them up and wipe off the counter.

"Ten years ago, back when I first started my podcast, I recorded an episode on the Vanderhilt case. I was convinced it was murder."

"That's true," I said. "I listened to that episode." I didn't mention that I'd listened to it for the first time today.

"Well, after I released that episode, I received an envelope and a note. Stop investigating. And five thousand dollars. So I stopped."

CHAPTER 18

PODCAST CONFESSIONS AT THE COZY CORNER

DETECTIVE DEXTER PUSHED his glasses up the bridge of his nose and then put his hands on his hips. "Someone paid you off to stop investigating?"

Jenny pushed a curl out of her eye. "Yes, I guess so."

I was confused. Jenny had the reputation of being a hard-nosed, albeit pushy, investigator who would stop at nothing to solve a crime."Why did you take the money and stop?"

Jenny's happy-go-lucky shell melted off like the hard shell on an ice cream cone on a hot day. She sat down and put her face in her hands. When she looked up, tears dragged her eyeliner down into two straight lines.

"I feel so bad about it, but it turned out to be the best decision for my life."

Dexter pulled a chair out and sat facing her. "No judgment here, just tell us what happened."

"Nothing really. I recorded one podcast on the

Vanderhilts, then I received the money and the note. I didn't record another episode on the subject. You have to understand. I was twenty years old, a college student, recording a podcast in a closet. Not a walk-in closet like Harper's, a tiny, you-can-barely-get-inside closet. That money helped me really get my podcast started."

"That's history, now. What I want to know is, did you notice anyone following you?" Dexter said, thinking like a detective.

"Maybe making sure you did what they asked?" I asked, thinking like a murder mystery writer. There's always someone following the protagonist when she gets close to the truth.

Jenny took her face out of her hands and sat up. "Come to think of it, yes. I told my mom about it but she didn't approve of me podcasting about murder, so she said I was creeping myself out."

It had been ten years. Was it possible for her to remember what he looked like? Also, how much has that person changed his looks in the past ten years?

Zoe said, "I have pictures of pretty much everyone in town. Maybe we could meet tomorrow and you could go through them."

"Everyone in Evergreen Heights has been involved in a crime?" she said incredulously, wiping her eyes with the tissue I'd given her.

"I have a studio where I do family portraits, plus I work for the paper. It's a small town," she explained. "I have…"

"Multiple streams of income," Jenny finished for her.

"Yes," Jenny, Sage, and I said in unison.

Dexter stood and shook his head. "You three are something else."

"Aren't we?" Jenny said. "I think I've found my people."

Jenny raised both arms in the air and we three danced a victory dance. We stopped, breathless and she looked at me. "Is your aunt a realtor?"

"Yes." I grabbed my phone and shared her contact info as well as my own.

Jenny stated, "Let's go, Sage. Let's let Poindexter and Agatha Raisin leave for their date."

"They are staying here, so we should get out of here," Sage answered and then immediately cast me a look that said "I'm sorry! Me and my big mouth."

Jenny grinned. "Oh, Sister Boniface she is not."

It's not like that! A zap of heat which started in my toes, rose to the tip of my roots. I was sure my freckles were going to burst into flame and consume my face.

Sage came to my rescue by saying, "Who do you want to interview first?" as she pulled Jenny toward the door.

"I brought dinner," Dexter said.

He had. I hadn't noticed the brown paper takeout bag on the counter. We sat down at the table and ate together without the dish of tension served with last night's meal. I filled him in on my day. Holding baby Peregrine, plotting out a cozy mystery, my meeting with Edgar, researching the case with Sage, and finally Jenny Murder showing up in my bookstore.

He listened intently. "I'd say you've had a productive day."

He didn't say "You've done too much," like my mother or even my aunt would say.

He spoke to me like I was an adult without a crippling, debilitating disorder. Which gave me pause. I wondered how many of my 'isms' and habits were fed by my aunt and mother giving me bad advice. Not because they didn't love me, but because they did. Instead of helping me, the advice to not do too much or other well meaning advice had me serving the agoraphobia instead of breaking free.

And despite what people were saying about Gabrielle befriending me, I'd enjoyed spending time with her. She felt genuine and as if, for the first time in a long time, she was enjoying her life, not giving into the demands and dictates of her husband. I'm a bad friend, I suddenly thought. I haven't called her or checked on her, since she'd come to book club after being released on bail. I made a mental note to call her and check on her, maybe see if she wanted to go for a hike.

Dexter hadn't made much progress that day. He knew what Sage did about the murder weapon, but it didn't make any sense.

After we cleaned up from dinner and the coffee cups that had been left on my counter, we moved to the sectional and started a movie.

When I woke up at midnight, Dexter was still there and I was leaning on him. Should I move? The movie had ended long ago and the smart TV screen advertised apps and the latest movie you could watch for "free." I wanted to stay here, leaning on Dexter's shoulder, but my bladder disagreed. After telling my bladder to wait, it threatened to burst open and not only ruin the moment, but humiliate me with an accident I wouldn't recover from. *Ever.*

I put a hand down to push myself up, not realizing said hand was on his knee, not the couch.

"You're awake," he said.

Instead of answering, I heaved myself off the couch and made a quick exit to the guest bath. I barely made it. It was all the coffees I'd consumed today draining my body of all fluid. I'd need to rehydrate.

That's what I was thinking? There was a handsome man on my couch who was actually interested in what I had to say and not throwing advice at me like "Drink more water." "Are you sure you should be doing that?" "Remember your fears, always serve them."

Okay, my aunt and mother had never said the last one, but it felt as if they had. As I washed my hands, I peered at my puffy eyes in the mirror. I splashed some cold water on my face and pinched my cheeks. Wake up and say something intelligent when you go back out there.

"Sorry, I really had to pee," I said as soon as I walked out of the bathroom. Great, Harper. So intelligent.

"I need to go," he said. "Do you want to come down and arm the system?"

"Can you do it?" I asked. "I'm really out of it."

"I can tell," he said.

The romantic bubble we'd had earlier popped into a bladder-induced, sleep-deprived, drippy, stinky mess.

"Yes, I can arm the system, but don't I need the code to do that?"

I wrote the code on a sticky note from the crime board and shoved it toward him.

"I'm going to bed. I had a very nice time." I turned and headed up the stairs.

"Wait a minute," he said.

I turned toward him. In exactly three long strides, he was standing in front of me. He wrapped his arms around me and squeezed me in a woodsy spice-scented weighted blanket bear hug.

"I had a good time too." He kissed the top of my head and let go. "I'll take Rory out before I leave."

At the sound of his name, Rory perked up, and ran toward the door.

Ten minutes after Rory and Dexter left, Rory ran back up to the apartment, and I locked the door. The notification popped up on my phone that the building was armed. I brushed my teeth, changed into my pajamas, and two minutes later I was fast asleep.

When I awoke I felt rested and excited at the same time. I survived a mostly normal-ish date with Dexter. Jenny Murder was here in my hometown. I felt good about the cozy mystery I was writing. I sat down at my desk in my PJs, plopped a pod in the Keurig and turned on my computer.

I'd made the mistake of using a folder entitled "my book" when I wrote my first book. For some reason, five years ago, I thought that was a great idea. Or I thought the first book would be my only…. which got me thinking, if I'd changed in the past five years, as far as my writing career and perspective goes, what about the murderer? Did he change? Maybe there were two murderers.

My phone buzzed, interrupting my thoughts. I picked it up.

Jenny was calling me on FaceTime.

I pushed join, forgetting I was in my PJs and I hadn't tamed my hair down.

"Good morning Miss Marple." Jenny's chocolate curls bounced in a synchronized dance, not a mishmash of kindergarteners at a recital like mine.

"Sage says you are friends with Gabrielle," she said.

"Yes, I was going to call her today," I added to myself.

Jenny leaned over the sink and picked up a toothbrush."Do you think she'd be a guest on the podcast?"

I'd stopped listening when I realized the wallpaper that was her backdrop was the wallpaper in my old bathroom.

"Are you at my aunt's house?" I asked. "In my room?"

"Oh, yeah, when Sage introduced us last night, Aunt Mary offered for me to stay here until she found me a house."

"So, you're serious about staying?" I asked.

"Yes, I think so," she said. "I love your bedroom. This bathroom wallpaper is amazing."

"Thank you." I had picked it out myself. "I'll call Gabrielle. Maybe we could go for a hike later today and she could join us."

"Perfect," she said.

We talked for a few more minutes before we hung up and I got back to work for a few hours before I texted Gabrielle and asked her if she were up for a hike.

Sure!

Full disclosure Jenny Murder will be joining us.

What? I'm such a fan. Can't wait to talk to you and tell you what's been going on.

What?

It's about the murders.

CHAPTER 19
CHRISTMAS TREE FOREST SHOW DOWN - AWAY FROM THE COZY CORNER

I WROTE another chapter of my cozy mystery, *The Evergreen Enigma,* drank a quart of water with hydrate powder and went to the bathroom exactly four times before I showered. I lightly toweled my hair with a tee shirt, a curly girl's hair trick, before scrunching my curls with some curl cream.

I looked at myself in the mirror as I diffused my curls. So many things have changed in my life in the past few months. Not only had I started working with Edgar and made some progress in getting out of the Cozy Corner building, I'd also made friends and met a guy who I really liked.

I wrote mysteries for a living-ish. So I knew that everything going well meant that something was about to go wrong. Either someone we thought was innocent was going to do something horrific and stun us all, or we were going to find out some piece of information that unlocked the case. Hopefully, it was the latter. I didn't plan on doing something stupid like meeting the murderer in a parking garage, which was ridiculous because Evergreen Heights didn't have a parking garage.

You're freaking yourself out, Harper, I told myself in the mirror as I turned the dryer off. I set down the hair dryer and smacked my cheeks. Self-sabotage is not on your to-do list. Enjoy the day. I picked up my phone and opened the Bible app. I know there's a verse somewhere about fear and having a sound mind. It was about time I started filling my mind with good things instead of keeping it in a torrential storm of doubt, worry, and anxiety and saying a quick blanket prayer that I'd have a good day. I wasn't in elementary school anymore. I wasn't housebound anymore. Not completely anyway. It was time for me to own my faith and not rely on the fact that at one time I went to church with Aunt Mary.

For some reason, when I'd started experiencing panic attacks and couldn't attend church as a tween, I had adopted the erroneous belief that I wasn't for church. Some people say church isn't for me. The opposite had become true for me - I wasn't for church. Where do people with crippling anxiety fit into church when they can't attend? They're labeled backsliders. I still remember the first time I heard myself called that awful word.

I had been in high school, and although I didn't attend church, I had thought I'd try the weekly youth group.

When the adult greeter had met me at the door to sign me in, after I'd passed her, she had leaned over to her helper and had said, "It's so good to see Harper here, I was afraid she'd backslidden."

I had lasted exactly ten minutes in the service before I'd collapsed during a too-loud worship song.

I found the verse. 2 Timothy 1:7

God has not given unto me a spirit of fear, but of power and of love and a sound and a disciplined mind.

That's a great one to memorize and pray.

With Edgar's help, I'd come to the realization that I needed to peel apart the modern culture of the church and God. God didn't necessarily agree with the current views of the church. He loved me despite my body rebelling against me. I didn't know if I could ever attend the loud modern church but that didn't exclude me from heaven, did it? Would heaven be overwhelming for me?

Stop going down theological rabbit holes, Harper. Read the scripture. Study it and go downstairs to work.

The day flew by. Ashley and Clare did an amazing job with story hour and I learned more about ghost busters from Dominic and Theo while they set up. We sat at the coffee counter and while they sipped juices, I drank my first coffee of the morning.

"So first," Theo said as he jumped down, "you have to run round the room like this." He ran round the tables, bumping into exactly three chairs. "That charges the battery."

"Yeaaaah, mom says the game keeps you active. That's important," Dominic explained.

Theo scrunched up his face."Sometimes you get slimed."

"Yuck," I said and made a face.

"Not for real," Dominic laughed. "In the game."

After the two story hours, I went back to my apartment for my second writing session. I'd decided to write both books at the same time:

The Evergreen Enigma and ***Murder in the Neighborhood*** introducing my new mom-sleuth, Lila Thompson.

Working on two books at a time was a big no-no in the author world. But when had I ever listened to what the publishing world said?

Before I knew it, it was time for my hike with Jenny and Gabrielle. I changed into my hiking gear and went back downstairs to wait for Gabrielle to pick me up. I texted Sage and asked her to join us because she was still touchy about my relationship with Gabrielle. I thought that if she spent some time with her, she might start to see what I saw, someone genuine and not a threat. But that wasn't going to work for her, she had some other work to do.

Gabrielle pulled up. I ran out and hopped in. Jenny Murder said "Hello" from the backseat.

"I see you two have met," I said while stuffing my phone in a side pocket of my new pink trekker pants.

"Yep. She picked me up at your aunt's. I hope you don't mind that I'm staying there. I should have asked you. I'm sorry. Sometimes I'm a little overzealous. Compulsive."

I tightened the laces on my hiking boots."No, it's fine. I haven't been there for five years."

"Oh," she said with a confused expression. "Your aunt is wonderful. Apparently, she's filming episode two of her new show on the other side of town."

"Yes, that's why Sage couldn't join us," I explained. "She's taking photos and writing a story about it."

We pulled into the parking lot of Christmas Tree Forest. Gabrielle had hardly said a word, which wasn't like her. I wondered if Jenny's presence had anything to do with it.

"How have you been, Gabrielle?" I asked as we headed toward the trail.

Gabrielle smoothed her already-perfect, vibrant red bob. "I've been pretty well since those few nights in jail. Eustace posted bail, as you know.'"

I was confused. Why did she need Eustace's money? The Vanderhilt money was hers now. Wasn't it?

Jenny walked beside us, head up admiring the hemlock trees. "Wow, Harper, this forest is incredible," Jenny exclaimed. "After living in New York City, I forgot how magical a place like this can feel. The air is so fresh, and the quiet is almost surreal."

Good, Jenny was too busy admiring the dense foliage and towering hemlocks to interrogate Gabrielle. I was afraid she was going to pull out a mic and start pelting Gabrielle with questions.

"I agree. Take in a deep breath." The air was crisp, carrying the clean, slightly sharp scent of pine. I stopped sniffing the air to ask a question myself.

"Why didn't you use your money?" I asked. Great, Harper, you don't want Jenny to question her so you are. I stepped on a twig and it snapped loudly, reverberating in the tunnel of tree branches.

Gabrielle pulled out some lip balm and applied it before saying, "What? I don't have any money. Anyway, Eustace has been so kind."

Then it happened. The revelation I expected growing like dough rising to the top of the pan. Which also meant we were in danger.

"Shhhh," I said as I heard the same twig thwack loudly. "Someone is following us."

Jenny and I simultaneously grabbed Gabrielle by the arms and pulled her off the trail, hiding behind a giant boulder.

"This is the point in my investigation that someone follows me and threatens me because I'm getting close to the answers," Jenny whispered.

"Yes, just like in my books," I said.

Jenny stifled a laugh, despite the seriousness of the situation. "Well, yeah, but usually there isn't a ten year delay."

"But there was another murder," I reminded, peeking around the edge of the boulder to see if I could see who was following us.

"I think I know who sent me the money," Jenny said.

"I think I do too," I replied.

We both looked at Gabrielle. "Don't look at me. I don't know what you're talking about. I don't have any money."

"And why is that?" I asked.

"Didn't your husband own the estate?" Jenny whispered.

I peeked around the boulder again as a couple with a toddler in a carrier walked by.

"The coast is clear," I said. We stood and dusted the leaves off ourselves. I took a swig of my water and continued to stare at Gabrielle.

"Oh, you want me to tell you why I have no money.

Apparently," she ran her fingers through her hair freeing a brown oak leaf, "there's a clause in the will saying if I commit a crime or am arrested for one, the whole estate goes to the next surviving relative."

"Eustace," Jenny and I said at the same time.

"Yes, he gets everything, but he's been so sweet. He's going to let me stay at the estate through the trial." Gabrielle wiped a tear from her cheek. "Isn't Eustace kind?"

We'd moved back on the trail. As we continued to question Gabrielle, a whooshing sound to the left of me caught my attention and to my horror, Jenny crumpled to the ground.

"Hit the dirt," she yelled.

The bark of the hemlock beside me splintered.

Gabrielle and I "hit the dirt" and crawled on our hands and knees back to the same boulder we'd just come out from behind.

"I knew you'd figure it out eventually," Eustace said from the other side of the boulder. "You and your little mystery mind."

Another shot rang out. My brain had caught up with the fact that someone was shooting at us. Jenny's arm was bleeding. I pulled the bandana from my hair and wrapped it around her arm as tightly as I could and tied it. "It just grazed me. But it hurts like …"

"I thought I paid you off, Miss Murder. The agreement was that you stopped investigating." Another shot hit the boulder and ricocheted off. Eustace screamed.

"The dummy's gone and shot himself," Jenny said.

Why wasn't Gabrielle saying anything? I looked to

my right where she'd been seated exactly one second ago and she was gone.

I peered around the boulder again. She was tending Eustace's wound. His self-inflicted shoulder wound.

"Is it true?" she asked as she examined his shoulder.

"You killed Horace and blamed me so you could inherit the estate and the money."

"It should have been mine in the first place," he said. "Not some girl from the gutter. The Vanderhilts used to have standards."

I walked toward Gabrielle, eyeing the gun. This was the part when the falsely accused might do something stupid, like pick up the gun and shoot the killer. As if on cue, Gabrielle picked up the gun and pointed it at Eustace, who was now seated and leaning against a tree holding his shoulder.

"You were being so kind, but you were faking the whole time. I thought you cared," she said, her slender frame trembling.

Jenny stayed behind the boulder as I advanced.

I crept forward, one baby step at a time. "Gabrielle, you didn't commit any crime, so the estate is yours. If you shoot him, you lose it all."

"I don't care about the estate. I just wanted someone to care about me. Do you know what it's like to live with a man who beats you every day and tells you that you are worthless?"

Gabrielle sobbed, her arms shaking as she pointed the gun at Eustace's head.

After two more steps, I would be close enough to grab the gun. "Well, not the beating part, but yeah, my dad thinks I'm broken…"

She turned and swung the gun in my direction. "You weren't faking, were you Harper?"

"No, I wasn't." I didn't get to finish my explanation because Eustace raised both legs and kicked Gabrielle's knees, she fell forward and the gun fired. Blood oozed out of my shoulder as Eustace crawled over top of Gabrielle.

There was no "Here's what happened..." like the famous defective detective. There were three gunshot wounds. Three people on the forest floor in various states of bleeding while the one able bodied person lost the wrestling match to a murderer.

As Gabrielle gasped for breath, on her backside, with one hand supporting her like a kickstand on a bike, she said.

"You killed your brother and Maria, the housekeeper."

He huffed and held his self-inflicted wound. "I should have gotten the estate."

I held my shoulder. "That's why he stopped the renovation on your house."

"The hot tub," Jenny yelled from behind the boulder, "Wasn't it supposed to be put in by the old conservatory?"

"Yes, and that's where he buried the bodies."

"Shut up," Eustace said. "I'm going to kill you all."

"I don't think so," Dexter said, stepping out from behind a tree. "Drop the gun."

A few police officers swarmed out from behind the hemlocks.

Jenny stood. "I recorded everything!"

"How did you know to come?" I asked Dexter when

the paramedics were cleaning my slightly grazed shoulder.

"Jenny called 911," Dexter replied.

"Thank God, Eustace is a bad shot," he added as he studied Jenny and me, who both had shoulder wounds.

"Oh, no, Gabrielle fell and the gun discharged and shot me."

"Eustace shot me," Jenny said.

"Who shot him?" Dexter asked.

Gabrielle said, "He shot himself. The bullet ricocheted off the rock and hit him."

"I guess shovels are usually his weapon of choice," I added.

Gabrielle, Jenny, and I laughed. I think this was going to be the start of a great friendship.

"What did I miss?" Sage asked, popping out of the forest.

CHAPTER 20
FRIENDS, FOOD, AND FUTURE PROMISES AT THE COZY CORNER

THANKFULLY, none of the three women who Eustace had threatened to kill had any serious injuries. Gabrielle ripped her hiking pants when he pushed her forward into some sharp rocks and wrestled with her. My shoulder wound was a graze which felt like I'd shaved my dry skin and gotten a razor burn. Jenny's was the most serious. A graze but deeper than mine. The bullet had penetrated a layer of muscle and come through the other side.

"My war wound in the fight for justice" she called it.

With all of the violence on the trail, I expected myself to have an episode when I returned home. Turns out, I had a delayed reaction. Two days after the danger had passed, my anxiety kicked in, which Edgar assured me was perfectly normal. I spent the whole day in my apartment under my weighted blanket.

Ashley and Clare brought their kids up for a few minutes. Dominic insisted that he bring the iPad so he could demonstrate ghost busters to cheer me up. As we ladies munched cookies and sipped coffee Zoe had sent up, they filled me in on story hour. Dominic and Theo ran through the main floor yelling intermittently.

"See Harper, running gets your battery charged."

"Yeah, I see a ghost!"

Rory, thinking the running was code for playing with him, joined the boys, hopping over the reading chair in the corner.

"Come on, Rory, help us so we don't get slimed."

"I'm sorry," Clare said. "This is probably making it worse…" Her words trailed off. I knew people were uncomfortable with mental illness and she didn't know what to say.

"Actually, I'm loving this. I don't know why I've waited so long to invite you guys up here."

"I've had bouts of extreme anxiety," Ashley said. "With postpartum depression."

I smiled. "It's tough, right?"

At that moment, I didn't want to take the time to explain how agoraphobia worked, so I thanked her for sharing. Then I had a great idea. Maybe for the next book club selection, Edgar could choose a book that covered some aspects of mental illness that wasn't too science-y. He could lead the study, not only so the townspeople would stop thinking of me as a crazy hermit lady. Talking about mental illness would open the discussion and help, well, everyone.

After Clare, Ashley, and the kids left, with Dominic and Theo promising to give me another tutorial *next time,* I put my noise reducing headphones on and fell asleep for exactly two hours.

After my nap, I disassembled the murder board and

hoped I'd never need another one. I went upstairs to my office and wrote three chapters of the tenth mystery in the series, *The Evergreen Enigma*. By the time I finished writing, the sunlight was fading. I realized I hadn't eaten anything today except two cookies. I didn't feel like leaving my apartment.

As the darkness descended, I sank down into despair. My moment of "better" disappeared like a whiff of smoke, and in its place was the heavy weighted blanket of anxiety. I threw off the weighted blanket like it was poisonous.

My phone buzzed alerting me that Zoe had armed the building.

Aunt Mary texted me:

I'm downstairs, can you come down for a minute?

I'd fully expected Aunt Mary to check in by phone since they'd been filming her show all day. She'd been exhausted, and with the murder behind her, she could finally finish the Vanderhilt mansion.

Gabrielle now had full authority to do whatever her heart desired. She didn't desire a hot tub by the conservatory, which meant the show would wrap up next week with the reveal. She had decided to use the money to open a home for foster youth, which I'm sure made Eustace livid. Which no one cared about for one second. Eustace would spend the rest of his life in prison wearing an orange jumpsuit and no one would care that he was a Vanderhilt.

Jenny had spent the last few days interviewing people for the Crimecaster podcast. After the recent revelation of Eustace's true character, everyone had something to say.

Turns out, Eustace had only joined the historical society to cover up the murder of his brother and housekeeper, Maria. The two hadn't planned on leaving the country, just the mansion. After having given Eustace two million dollars, his brother Clive had been handing over the current house to his son so he could build his own modern house with his future bride, Maria. All of the information about his plan Jenny had gleaned from interviewing the employees at the Vanderhilt estate and company.

Lots of townspeople were upset at the restrictions Eustace had enforced when they were remodeling their historic homes. So Aunt Mary had a stack of complaints to deal with. My mother had fled the country once again. She only hung around for positive publicity and she certainly didn't want to clean up the mess Eustace had left behind.

Jenny was still living with my aunt and camping out in my bedroom. Sage was busy with the newspaper and her forensic photography job. Gabrielle had stopped by but she was busy with the last stages of the house designs as well.

I threw on some yoga pants and twisted my knotted hair up into a bun.

"Come on, Rory, let's go downstairs." I hoped Aunt Mary would walk him for me. He'd been cooped up with me all day except for the brief walks Zoe had taken him on.

I padded down the three flights to the main part of the bookstore in my slippers. It was dark.

Where was she? I stood next to the cafe counter and leaned over it to reach a light. Why was the counter covered with food? And why did it smell like my favorite bacon avocado burger here? I flipped on a small lamp on the counter.

"Surprise," Aunt Mary said from behind me. "I thought I'd bring you dinner. I didn't want to scare you."

"So you turned out all the lights?" I said.

"Well, there's a few more of us here, and we thought…"

My hand went to my messy bun and my gaze to my yoga pants. By "there are more of us," she meant Dexter? I couldn't be sure.

"I'll be right back. Can you walk Rory?" I didn't wait for a response but ran up three flights of stairs, opened my closet, grabbed a dress and changed quickly. I tamed down my messy bun to look a bit more intentional, shoved my feet into boots and flew back downstairs.

The lights were on. People were serving themselves from the buffet counter Aunt Mary had set up. The alarm notification was sent to keep me in the dark, so to speak.

Zoe, Sage, Jenny, Gabrielle, Dexter, Edgar and some of the other members of The Classics, plus Ashley and Clare sans children filled the space and my heart.

I hoped I didn't need to make a speech. Aunt Mary shoved a plate into my hands with my burger of choice and sweet potato fries. "I figured you haven't eaten all day."

"What is all this?" I asked.

"Just some friends gathering and having dinner,"

she said, enveloping me in a squeezy hug. "And celebrating your victories with you."

"The victory of staying in my PJs all day under a weighted blanket with waves of anxiety washing over me? That victory?"

Edgar patted me. "You've come a long way and it's not over yet. Don't think that one day like today means you are back to the beginning. You'll feel better tomorrow."

The next hour flew by as I chatted with everyone and ate until I thought my stomach would pop. Bea, the baker, had sent over a carrot cake, my favorite.

I only spoke to Dexter for exactly two minutes. But in those two minutes, I had a promise of a future.

"What are you doing tomorrow afternoon?" he asked.

"I don't have any plans."

"How about spending it with me?"

"Yes," I said.

———

What to read next:

Crimecaster Cold Case: A Christian Cozy Mystery in the Pursuit of a Serial Killer (Cozy Corner Mysteries Book 2)

Copyright © 2024 by Kathleen Guire

All rights reserved.

No part of this book may be reproduced in any form or by any electronic or mechanical means, including information storage and retrieval systems, without written permission from the author, except for the use of brief quotations in a book review.

Cover by Beckanddot

ABOUT THE AUTHOR

Kathleen Guire is the mother of seven, four through adoption, NiNi of fourteen, former National Parent of the Year, author, teacher, and speaker. She loves connecting with readers through her website (Kathleen guireauthor.com).

For more information,
about Kathleen, check out her website and follow her
on social media!
www.kathleenguireauthor.com
kathleenguire@gmail.com
https://linktr.ee/kguire

FOR MORE INFORMATION,

ABOUT KATHLEEN, CHECK OUT
HER WEBSITE AND FOLLOW HER
ON SOCIAL MEDIA!

www.kathleenguireauthor.com

kathleenguire@gmail.com

https://linktr.ee/kguire

ALSO BY KATHLEEN GUIRE

What to read next:

Crimecaster Cold Case: A Christian Cozy Mystery in the Pursuit of a Serial Killer (Cozy Corner Mysteries Book 2)

www.ingramcontent.com/pod-product-compliance
Lightning Source LLC
Chambersburg PA
CBHW060316310726
48976CB00007B/2346